Femaestus

Dani Kirk

Femaestus

DEDICATION

Dedicated to my family, friends, fiancé and fledglings

Femaestus

1

The sea was flat, black and still. So still. The only thing to break it was the small boat slicing its way through like a slow sharp knife. The men on the boat were silent as they peered out into the blackness with wide frozen eyes. Heavy curtains of fog shrouded them intermittently before clearing again for a short distance. The eight men were huddled close in the tiny wooden frame but none of them made a sound, except for the faint chattering of teeth emitting from a few of them. The youngest and smallest man, Buddy, had a wet nose and suddenly sneezed.

"Shhh! Are you nuts?" spat Croner through gritted teeth, "you want to let them know we're here do you?" Buddy cowered into his scratchy red blanket as all the other men darted a glare at him. He hadn't meant to sneeze. He was just as scared as the rest of them. This was his second trip across the water - his first one having been that morning – but it had been daylight then and, although still terrifying, was now exacerbated by the pitch black of night. Buddy looked up at the stars twinkling above which he could only get a glimpse of now and again when the mist cleared. He judged by the position of the stars that they mustn't be far from the first stop off now – his was the third which meant he was nearly home. He released a breath of relief that curled up in the frosty air above him, making undulating patterns before his eyes. It was tantalising and, mixed with the gentle swaying of the boat, Buddy began to feel almost relaxed.

Then a noise rang out. At first, Buddy thought it was the echo of his sneeze returning to him, delayed and higher in pitch, but with the second sound Buddy and the other seven men knew immediately what it was.

"Femaestus," whispered the oldest man on the tiny boat. Buddy began to quiver. Surely not? Surely he wouldn't encounter them on his first trip to The Mainland. The sound came again and Buddy felt terror strike his body, filling his eyes with tears and loosening his bladder. He tried to hold both in but began to sob as he soiled himself. "Pull yourself together, man," grunted the old boy. The sound began a third time but this time louder and merging into the following sound. A song. A beautiful song, Buddy thought. The mellow tempo and sombre tones caressed his ears and stroked the back of his neck. The womanly voice flowed as smoothly as pure running water, enchanting the men on the boat. Then Buddy shook his head. 'Don't let it fool you,' he reminded himself and in that moment the song ceased. Silence filled the air for all of five hopeful seconds before a big black figure leapt from the water and across the boat with such great speed that it took a moment for the men to realise that it had taken the oldest man down with it.

"To hell with this! Come on you pansies! Get rowing!" Croner sounded angry but Buddy knew it was fear that was bubbling in his throat and spewing out of his mouth. As Croner grabbed an oar, a gnarly webbed hand seized the other end just below the surface of the water. The hand was mouldy; its fingers were long and sharp. Croner yanked on the oar and the hand popped out of the water. For a second Buddy saw it change. As it hit the icy night air, the skin turned smooth and glistened in the faintest moonlight. The fingers became rounded and looked as soft as a baby's. Then it tugged back with incredible strength and Croner didn't let go. He was flung overboard. Water sprayed up into the boat. Some landed on Buddy but then he realised something that didn't make sense to him at first. The water was warm. He wiped a bit off the back of his hand.

"It's blood." He whimpered, barely audible.

Suddenly, in quick succession, more dark figures left the water and swept the boat clean of life. The fearful cries of grown men echoed through the air but they were helpless out in the waters, they simply faded to nothing as bodies were dragged below the surface. Splashing and chaos surrounded the boat and Buddy could hardly make out what was going on. Other men had been grabbing oars, lanterns, anything they could use to protect themselves. Sticks and knives were flailing around in the air in a jumbled scene of trepidation and confusion until finally there was calmness and Buddy realised he was the last man left. His heart froze in his chest as he made out the black silhouette of a flaky tail rise out the water, inches from his small helpless face. It smelt rotten. It smelt like death. The tail ducked back under without making a sound. Tranquillity again. The water was as flat and still as it had been moments earlier and for a brief second Buddy couldn't believe his luck. Before he knew it however, the water broke and the body of a woman came soaring towards him, accompanied by a scream that splintered the sea air. The last thing he saw was her hungry demonic eyes and dripping skin as she pulled him down to the depths.

2

It was Arik's birthday. He came into the kitchen to see his mother, Vivienne, leaning over the table, blocking whatever she was doing. From the back he could see that she had her thin eggshell dress on with the dainty white flowers that she wore for special occasions. Tied in a knot round her waist was the band of her off white apron which she wore every day. He guessed it made her feel busy, gave her a purpose, as if she was wearing a uniform.

"Arik! Happy fifteenth birthday my boy!" She spun around and hugged him, her small egg-shaped stomach pressing into his concave one. Her auburn hair brushed his cheeks. It smelled musty, probably because they didn't have access to much shampoo, but it smelled like home and Arik inhaled her essence deeply. "I know it's not much but I made you a cake." Arik peered behind her to the table where two loaves of bread were pushed together with a lumpy layer of white icing spread unevenly over them both. A single candle sprouted from the middle but not like your typical birthday candle, but one of those thick old red Christmas ones from years ago with a tiny flame dancing on top. Arik smiled. He appreciated his mother's effort and he wanted it to show on his dark olive face so he stretched his lips into the biggest smile he could muster.

"Thanks, mum. It's perfect." Arik should have been happy that it was his birthday but he wasn't. Soon his father, Morgan, came into the room and reminded him why. He clapped his hands heavily then ruffled Arik's soot black hair. Arik got his dark features from his father. From his varnished wood coloured skin to his silky dark hair and plain black eyes. It always amazed Vivienne how dark Arik's skin was considering he rarely went outside.

"Fifteen today, son. One more year and you'll be coming out with me to The Mainland." Both Arik and his mother had no idea why Morgan had decided that reminding everyone of what was to happen in a year's time was the best way to start the morning of Arik's birthday. Perhaps he didn't want everyone getting too happy and comfortable, he liked to keep people in touch with reality. Arik gulped and his mother's eyes widened but neither of them responded. The awkward silence that followed was thankfully soon broken by Arik's little brother Kai entering the kitchen. Kai also had the dark skin and eyes like his brother and father but Kai had the reddish hair like their mother.

"Hey Arik, happy birthday! What do you want to do today? Dad's home so we could go play cards out on the deck! Or do some painting out there? Or-" Before Kai could even finish or Arik could open his mouth to respond, Vivienne barked,

"No! You know I don't want you playing out on the deck!" She slammed the tea towel she was holding down on the table and placed her other hand on her hip, exercising authority.

"Woah, hey, calm down," Morgan soothed, "They need to do something different now and again Vivienne, it's Arik's birthday after all and like Kai said, I'm right here today if there's any trouble." Arik looked at Kai and Kai looked at Vivienne with the biggest dopey pleading eyes Arik had ever seen someone do.

"*Please,* Mum, " he begged.

"Fine," Vivienne huffed reluctantly after a short pause, "but just keep your voices down." Vivienne didn't want to keep her children locked inside. She often felt as though she was holding her boys prisoner in their own home and it pained her to keep them cooped up. But they were all she had and their safety was paramount. The words of her husband relieved her but also irritated her. How could he be so calm about them playing outside? Her anger was softened when she looked at her youngest, Kai, who grinned at Arik with a toothless smile. Arik was sure his younger brother should have all his teeth by now at twelve years old but maybe malnourishment didn't help with that. All of Arik's teeth had been through for years but they weren't exactly sparkling white. Toothpaste was a rarity and their father didn't often bring it back from The Mainland. Arik felt Kai tugging on his sleeve and the boys decided to act fast before their mother changed her mind and so picked up a pack of playing cards each and went out onto the deck together, both grabbing a handful of Arik's bread cake on the way out.

3

The swing doors throughout the hospital flung open as the nurses crashed down the corridors rushing Lana to the delivery ward. Purple blurs remained in her aching eyes from the lights that invaded them from overhead. There was a lot of fuss and commotion. Lana felt weak. Contractions were slicing through her stomach now at short intervals, hardly giving her a chance to breathe. She had heard childbirth was difficult but this searing pain felt like she was being stabbed repeatedly over and over again. She felt as though she might pass out from the pain. Her left arm was heavy and slung over the edge of the cold hard bed where a drip penetrated her skin. The area around the shiny spike was mottled mauve and crimson and a small gaping hole was the evidence of rushed and misplaced needlework. The pain bolted through her body again. It struck the walls of her womb and caused her stomach muscles to clench so tight she felt as though they were tangling into knots. The outside of her head felt as heavy as lead but the inside felt light and airy. Tiny black spots started appearing in her eyes and she knew she was going to lose consciousness. The alarmed voices of the nurses in the room began to quieten and muffle and the lights above her began to blur and dim. Her eyelids fell shut. Lana fainted.

When she woke, Lana felt groggy and her head throbbed. She peeled open her crusty eyes and tried to adjust to the bluish artificial light above her. She looked around. An empty white room encased her. A single mirror on the wall to her left reflected her pasty ashen skin and dry tired eyes. She was gaunt from head to toe. She rubbed her stomach. Then it all came flooding back to her - where she was and why she was there. She still felt weak but a mother's love can muster up almighty strength and she found the power to shout for a nurse. Within minutes a nurse with a doubtful face entered the room. Lana could feel her apprehensiveness permeate the air.

"Where's my baby?" Lana whispered, a lump forming quickly in her throat.

"I'm afraid we have some bad news," the nurse looked to the floor and held her own hands, "it was a girl."

"So!? So where is she!?" Even though Lana knew what this meant, she still wanted her baby. "Miss, I think you know where she is. Now, when you are better you can leave the hospital." Lana's blood began to boil beneath her skin. Her heart felt enlarged and withered at the same time. She felt sick deep within her stomach and the lump in her throat was barely allowing her to catch a breath. She clenched the bed sheets in her fists as a tear fell from her eye and traced her lower lashes. It was followed by many more that hissed against her burning red cheeks. Anguish rose up from her womb and left her lips in the form of a tormented scream.

"No!" she howled, "No! Give me my daughter please! I beg you!" Lana tried to pull herself out of the bed and grab at the nurse but she was restrained. The nurse just apologised quietly under her breath, turned on her heel and sauntered back out of the room leaving Lana screaming and turning red as though blood may pour from her ears and eyes any moment.

Hours passed and Lana lay in her bed silently, drenched in her own tears. Her face was sodden but her lips were split and dry. She felt lost. Empty. She stared at the blank white wall in front of her. She stared and she stared. She couldn't think. Her mind felt damaged, her heart crushed. She was so busy gazing at the wall in her own numb world that she almost didn't notice a doctor enter the room. He came up to her bed with a clipboard and pen in hand.

"Hi there. I have just come in to let you know that you'll be well enough to leave the hospital tomorrow. Is there anything I can get you?"

In that moment, the words 'my daughter' didn't even enter Lana's head, let alone leave her mouth. She knew it was a lost cause. This didn't mean she had accepted it but simply that she understood it. She understood how the world was. She understood the risks of having a baby and the consequences of having a girl. She imagined her tiny baby daughter with a lovely soft button nose and cute blue eyes. She imagined her dainty arms and podgy tummy. Then she imagined her metallic scales on her fish tail. Then Lana grabbed the pen out of the doctor's hand and rammed it into her jugular.

4

Arik had beaten his brother at five out of six games of cards already and they had only been outside a short while. Although it was exciting being outside, the novelty was quickly wearing off and playing card games was becoming tediously boring.

"I wish there was something more fun to do for my birthday," Arik sighed, but he hadn't really meant to say it out loud.

"Well there is something," Kai replied, sheepishly. Arik eyed him suspiciously. "Remember that day a few months back when we last came outside and you were painting and you told me to leave you alone? Well I went round the back of the deck with dad's binoculars and saw a cove at the edge of the mainland and in the cove was the most beautiful thing I have ever seen! Maybe we could go sit round the back and look for it again?"

"What was it?"

"Don't know."

"Yes you do, what was it?"

"I don't know what it was!" Kai yelled.

"Shhh!" hissed Arik, "Mum told us to keep our voices down remember? Come on then if it'll keep you quiet let's go." Kai smiled up at his brother and got up and unhooked their dad's binoculars off the rack outside.

Arik and Kai sat round the back of the deck. Almost an hour passed and Arik could feel himself getting restless.

"There's nothing in that cove, Kai," he sighed. They had found the cove through the binoculars almost immediately. It was easy to see the edge of The Mainland when you could zoom in and there was a perfectly direct line between all the other stilt houses that allowed them a great view. The cove was a dark hole against the deep cliff face where white foam lapped at the bottom and a few birds perched on the crags up the top. But there was nothing exciting happening in there and certainly nothing beautiful.

"Just wait a bit longer *please*," Kai begged his older brother. Arik huffed and rolled his eyes. He lay back with his arms behind his head and stared up at the sky. The sky was the most beautiful thing in his opinion. Light blue with faint wisps of white smudged across it. It looked so open, so free, so safe. A bird glided gently across his view. He felt soothed. Then Kai punched his thigh.

"Arik!" He whispered excitedly, "there it is!"

Arik hauled himself up onto his elbows and took the binoculars off of Kai who was holding them so eagerly in his face. He pressed the cold black plastic against his eye sockets and tried to adjust. At first he couldn't even find the cove, scanning the entire cliff face so zoomed in made it difficult to navigate. Then he caught the birds on the crags he had seen earlier so he lowered his view a minute amount. Then he saw it. Or rather, he saw *her*. At first all he could make out were copious amounts of wet black hair that looked weighty where it was so saturated but then she turned her head slightly and her alluring face came into view. Her milky skin was flawless and her eyes were large and as deep and as blue as the sea. Her pale pink lips looked moist and soft. Arik lowered his binoculars some more. Her hair continued down her unclothed body but he could make out from the side the shape of an ample breast. He felt an urge to touch it. He imagined cupping the wet breast in his hand and it being firm but malleable at the same time. He shook his head and lowered the binoculars some more. Something was shining. At first it looked like the bottom half of a dress, embellished with emeralds, was clinging to her waist. Then he realised that it *was* her waist and it continued down. He followed it, again moving his binoculars tiny amounts at a time. The bright emerald colour gradually became merged into a bottle green and became duller at the point that it touched the water but her iridescent tail emerged from the other end and it was the most breath-taking thing he had ever laid his eyes on. The sheer size of the tail astounded him and its grandeur and elegance left him in awe. As she waved it slowly in the air, droplets falling from its underside, it caught the sun and the golden light reflected into Arik's eyes. He felt mesmerised.

"Arik! Arik! It's my turn now, let me look!" For a moment, Arik wondered how long he had been staring. Luckily, his little brother had shaken him from his enchantment and his senses came soaring back to him.

"Kai, it's a Femaestus! You know that! We shouldn't be out here staring at her. She could call for others if she spots us. It could be dangerous!" As soon as the final word left his mouth, a deep voice echoed from around the corner of the house.

"What could be so dangerous boys?" Arik was now aware of his dad's footsteps edging closer from round the side of the house. Kai quickly sat on the binoculars. Morgan appeared at the back of the deck.

"Erm, nothing," both the boys replied, terribly obviously lying. Morgan chuckled.

"Well my binoculars are missing, you boys are hiding round the back here and the most dangerous thing in these waters are Femaestus, so how about we stop lying to your old man and you tell me where you spotted one." The boys froze. They knew their dad was wise and there was no lying to him. Arik swallowed hard then opened his mouth ready to speak when Kai got there first.

"It was nothing dad, honest. We were just saying it *could* be dangerous *if* we saw one."
Arik was stunned at this outright lie that just left his brother's mouth - so stunned in fact that he found himself unable to talk. Morgan eyed them suspiciously and then said, "Fine. I don't believe you boys would lie to me. Come on now, I think it's time to go inside, that's enough for one day," and turned and started making his way back to the front of the house.

"Ok dad, we'll be in in a minute!" Kai called after him.

"Why did you do that?" Arik managed to utter.

"Do what?" Kai's innocent eyes bulged out of his face trying to look confused.

"You know what, why did you lie to dad about the Femaestus?"

"Please Arik, don't tell. She's like my little secret. I love to watch her. Please don't tell dad because he might… make her go away." Kai's face was full of worry and sadness. Arik could see it written on his skin. His little brother was begging him. Arik thought about his words and looked at his innocent face. His naivety worried him.

"I won't tell him today. But I will one day. Femaestus aren't a joke Kai. They're not beautiful. They're not something to stare at. You'll have to grow up and realise one day."

As Arik said that, he felt a pang of guilt rip through him as he remembered how drawn in by the fish-tailed woman he was himself, and how he longed to touch her and how he might've not ever stopped staring at her if Kai hadn't been there. He shook his head and internally also told himself to grow up.

5

The room where a lady called Lana had come in to give birth that morning had been mopped up of her blood and her body had been removed and taken down to the morgue. The nurse who'd been looking after her was called Penelope. Penelope was a quaint woman with small shoulders and narrow hips. Her face was strangely round, in comparison to the rest of her tiny frame, and was covered with faint freckles that began as a cluster about her nose and dispersed out towards her hair and jaw lines. Her hair was of a matching colour to her chestnut freckles and was scooped back in a low bun. There was nothing exciting about Penelope and, although she did care, she hadn't much of a personality either, which is why she appeared so indifferent when she had been the one who had to tell Lana the news that she had given birth to a girl. News that once would have filled people with glee and joy and caused tears of happiness to explode from a new mother's eyes. News that now no woman wants to hear. News that now sets fire to the empty womb and fills the air with sharp black butterflies. Something caught Penelope's eye. Lying on the floor just below the bed was a tatty old bracelet made of frayed rope. It was adorned with tiny discoloured shells of different shapes. It must have belonged to Lana. Perhaps it had meant something to her. She would never know now. She picked it up carefully and placed it in her pocket. Penelope stared into the white room. It was silent and clean as though nothing had happened. She sighed and made her way up to the laboratory.

She pushed open the big steel door to the lab. A faint smell of burning was in the air mixed with cleaning chemicals and steam. Travis, the scientist who ran the lab, was doubled over a petri dish doing something very intricately with a pipette. Penelope cleared her throat.

"Travis, sir, we had another one this morning. Caucasian mother, 24 years old, only illness known was asthma, do you want this one for testing? She's currently down in the tank." Travis continued to do whatever he was doing and didn't even show a sign of response. She waited a few moments, eyeing his reedy spine that arched into his white lab coat and watching his dry ash hair scrape against his shoulders. She thought he looked frailer and more aged than he should. Eventually she spoke again.

"Travis, sir, I said we've-"

"Yes, I heard you!" Travis cut Penelope off. "I have told you. I need to find another way to test for a cure. I am not having one more of those, those *things* near me ever again after last time."
Penelope looked down to Travis' bandaged up left hand on which only two fingers remained.

"But sir, they are only babies." Travis threw his pipette to the floor and swung round on his chair. He seized Penelope with his right hand while shoving his bloody left bandaged hand in her face.

"Only babies you say? How many babies do you know can remove three of your fingers with their teeth!? Oh, that's right, none - unless they are FEMALE. These are not just babies Penelope, they arc monsters. They are born with razor teeth and the strength of an adult and a TAIL. And, and," Travis loosened his grip on Penelope and took a couple of steps backwards, his voice calming to a sob, "and it's my entire fault that this came about anyway. And I cannot rest until they are gone. The damage they do. The lives they have taken. I thought I was doing good Penelope. I thought I was doing what was right." Penelope allowed Travis to slump into her arms as his tears dampened her chest. She thought about reassuring Travis. She thought about reminding him of all the good things that had come from his work. Instead, she pushed him back onto his chair, folded her arms and looked down at the weak broken man in front of her.

"So, what do you want me to do with her?"

"Throw it in the lake like the rest of them."

"But Travis, it's still a-"

"It's not a baby and yes it will die, just like the rest of them. Now get rid of it. The sooner we rid the earth of these godless creatures the better." Penelope looked down at the floor. It didn't matter, Travis hadn't looked her in the eye the whole time he spoke of chucking them in the lake anyway. For one whole year now, girls had been born with fish tails in place of legs. For one whole year, Penelope had gotten away with being the one to throw them in the lake outside. But as it was now the law, due to the danger posed by these things, to dispose of them, her supervisors were watching her closely to see if she could handle the job. She turned and clasped the big steel door handle. She paused for a second. She wasn't sure why. Maybe she was hoping Travis would change his mind about dumping the baby but he sat silent. With that, she heaved open the door and headed for the basement.

Down in the basement it was cold and smelled like a sewer; a fishy sewer. It was never like this before but, due to the epidemic, a reinforced tank had been installed down there. It wasn't a glass tank but a heavy-duty metal one with walls seven feet high. It was quiet. Penelope's footsteps echoed against the cold steps leading up to the top of the tank. She peered over into the water. At first, she couldn't make anything out due to the murkiness but as her eyes adjusted she caught a glimmer of something flitting about beneath the surface. There it was again. Small green flashes reappearing in the water as if a row of twinkling Christmas lights lined the bed of the tank. Penelope leaned over some more to get a better look. The water was so dirty. She pushed her body forward until her nose was almost touching the surface. Then something extraordinary happened to Penelope. The flashes stopped and instead a big green glow shone constant from deep within the water right below her face. Then, as the water settled to almost flat, a small baby hand reached slowly out of the water and held her jaw. The touch was cold but it was so soft, so gentle. Soon the other hand protruded from the water and also held her face. Penelope felt at ease. How could Travis call these things monsters? It was just a baby! Suddenly an alarm pierced the air and red flashing lights rolled around the basement walls. The tiny hands sprung back into the water and Penelope jumped back. As she did so something else in the tank caught her eye. It must have been kicked up by the baby fish-tailed girl as she panicked. Penelope looked closer. A door behind her flung open and two guards came in.

"Excuse me miss, one of the doctors has gone missing and with everything so high risk we are sounding the alarm until we find him. Have you seen Doctor Koleski?" As soon as the guard finished what he was saying, Penelope realised what it was floating towards her in the tank. It was a chewed up hand.

"I think I may have just found him."

6

Six months passed since Arik's birthday and one day Morgan's friend Hugo came over. Arik never really liked Hugo. He wasn't sure why but then he wasn't sure about a lot of things. Something about Hugo bothered him. Maybe it was his wiry orange moustache or maybe it was the way he wore his furry checked coat off his shoulders, as if the cold sea air didn't bother him, but mostly Arik thought that it was the way he spoke that really irritated him. He had this joyous way of talking about everything that Arik didn't quite believe and it was as if he used flamboyant hand gestures to convince you that whatever he was saying was true. Arik definitely didn't like him but he was dad's friend and nobody was really in the position to pass on friends, especially ones that would risk the journey to see you.

Arik sat on the floor with his brother to help him do some maths and pretend he wasn't listening to his dad and Hugo but he was. They were talking about all sorts of adult things and Arik decided he should start learning as much as possible to prepare him for going to work on The Mainland. He figured eavesdropping was allowed if it was educational.

"Not long now till the boy makes his journey with us then, Morg," Hugo spouted in his overly friendly tone that Arik despised.

"Not long at all. He'll make for a fine worker, he's got a good head on his shoulders," Arik smiled to himself inside at this praise from his dad, "I just wish he didn't have to take the journey at all though." His father's voice brimmed with sadness as he uttered this.

"I know what you mean," sighed Hugo, "but that's life now unfortunately." A silence followed as Morgan sat there and thought about when this way of living *wasn't* life.

He remembered back to the days when he first bought a house with his wife, Vivienne. He remembered how beautiful she looked as she stood smiling in the doorway of their new home. They were both so young then. Morgan remembered scooping his fresh-faced wife off of her feet and carrying her into their house that they had worked hard to get the money to buy. He thought about how they used to talk about starting a family. Then he remembered the day Vivienne told him she was pregnant for the first time. He recalled his heart filling with glee and tears of happiness welling in his eyes at the same time. There had been a lot going on in the news at that time about climate change and rising sea levels and danger and warnings were flooding the streets as quickly as the water was but they had been so wrapped up in their happiness, so full of excitement, they had barely taken any notice. Some years after Arik was born, news had gotten out about girls being born with fish tails. The news stated that they were born hostile and a law had come into place that all baby girls were to be 'disposed of' immediately following birth. This news filled Vivienne and Morgan with trepidation as they had just found out they were to have their second baby soon and with this new infection causing foetus' not to grow their bottom halves until the final month of pregnancy, there was no way of knowing what sex their baby would be until it was too late. Ultrasounds became obsolete and abortions were not an option by month nine – it was safer to go full term. Fortunately though for Morgan and Vivienne, three years after Arik was born, Kai came along – another son. Morgan remembered the relief he felt when Kai was born – more relief than happiness. This made him feel guilty. What made him feel even guiltier was that there was something he remembered even more clearly about the day Kai was born than the birth of his son. When they got home, there was a letter addressed to their house, directly from the government. With shaking hands, Morgan opened it and read the following:

"We are writing to you to inform you that, due to unforeseen changes in the sea level rise, all tier three residents must also be evicted and moved to stilt housing with immediate effect. Please find enclosed information of where your new home will be and how to get there. You have 48 hours to remove yourself from The Mainland. If you do not comply, the water will rise up over your current home and you will become endangered. DO NOT attempt to move further into The Mainland as this has been reserved for the higher tier and more valued individuals of society. If you do, soldiers will be sent in to forcibly prevent you by any means necessary."

Morgan had been so sure that they would be safe. They lived quite far into land in a reasonably pleasant area. The rising sea levels must have gotten worse than previously anticipated. How could he be expected to up and leave his home with his wife and his two sons, one of which had just been born, within 48 hours? Or ever? After much deliberation and discussion with Vivienne, they reluctantly decided to comply and began packing their things. They were to catch a small bus down to the water's edge and from there be taken by boat to their new 'home'.
Morgan remembered three-year old Arik sitting on his lap excitedly, looking out of the bus window and asking questions which were all just a blur to Morgan. He remembered looking at his wife cradling their baby boy on the cramped bus. He could see fear in her protective eyes. He remembered placing his hand on her thigh and reassuring her with the bravest façade he could muster up plastered onto his face. It was a bumpy ride on the bus. Arik kept screeching with happiness over every bump. It had all happened so quickly. Their life was going to change forever.

Eventually, Morgan snapped out of his day dream and just calmly said,
        "You're right, Hugo, this is life now but I guess there really is no point in us being bitter about it all. Things will get better. I have heard the few rich and intelligent folk

left on The Mainland are working on a cure for the girls right now. Plus, the work we go and do every day, manually extending The Mainland, eventually that'll mean we can move back."

"They've been working on a cure for the Fems for fifteen years, Morg! The guy that caused it all in the first place was working on it for the first year or so. If anyone was going to know a cure surely it would've been him! No, there's no hope for change. This is life now." Hugo was still strangely smiling as he said all this. It was sort of an angry smile through gritted teeth. Arik noticed that he made no comment on Morgan's suggestion of potentially returning to The Mainland one day.

Arik felt dark. His shoulders felt heavy as if some kind of pressure was weighing him down. He hadn't known any other life but when he heard the adults talk about 'how it was before' it made him feel down and strangely jealous. He had never known a life full of the things he had overheard his parents talk about. He had never had a walk in the park or a day at school. He had never gotten a lolly from the ice cream van or played football with his friends. He had never gone for a swim despite being surrounded by water.

He had never met a girl that wasn't his mum.

The girl from the cove suddenly entered Arik's mind. He hadn't met a girl but he'd *seen* one, back on his fifteenth birthday. He wondered if Kai had seen her since. It was possible as they had been doing a lot of studying at different times and with his mum always seeming to have other things on her mind, Kai had become quite good at slipping under the radar. Arik decided to consult his brother quietly,

"Kai, you know what we saw in the cove on my fifteenth birthday?" Arik lowered his voice even more, "well I was just wondering if you had seen it since?" He felt angry with himself for calling her an 'it' but he knew that it was the right thing to do. Kai shrugged his shoulders. "Tell me, Kai!" Arik grabbed his little brother's arm as he half shouted, half whispered. Kai looked at him with big sad eyes and Arik realised this wasn't the best approach. Calmly, he then asked, "I was just wondering if you had seen it again, Kai. I was just interested. You can tell me, I am your brother." Kai turned slowly to face the floor.

"If you stop calling her '*it*' then I might tell you." He sulked.

"Okay, okay. Have you seen *her?*" Arik held back a sigh.

"Of course I have. I watch her at least once a week. I told you, she's *my* special secret."

Arik was stunned. Although part of him wanted Kai to say yes, he didn't actually consider that he might. He wasn't sure how he felt about his brother's 'special secret' – surely it wasn't jealousy, was it? While he contemplated this, Kai spoke up,

"She watches me now too. She started swimming towards me the other day but didn't get very far because something scared her away."

That's when Arik knew that what he felt for his brother was fear.

"Kai, listen to me, you have GOT to STOP. If you keep this up, you'll put yourself in danger. You have to stop."

"No!"

"Shhh! Please Kai. You can't have your special secret any more I'm afraid."

"Yes I can and I will!"

"Kai, she could *kill* you! Do you understand that? If she doesn't, dad will."

"Dad doesn't know."

"He will when I tell him."

"No Arik, no please, please. Don't tell Dad."

"Promise you won't go to the back of the deck to watch it – *her* – anymore then!" Kai lowered his head and sniffed. Arik knew he was upset, on the brink of crying. Under his breath, Kai just squeaked,

"Promise."

7

The remainder of the body parts that previously belonged to Doctor Koleski were fished out of the tank. The smell made Penelope heave. A black bin bag was filled with chunks of mangled flesh, shreds of clothing, some splintered bones and the chewed hand. The cleaners that had come down to collect it all left with the bag but the two guards remained in the basement with Penelope.

"Are you okay, Miss?" The only response Penelope could manage was a slight nod. "Can I ask what it was you were doing down here anyway?"

"I, I was supposed to be disposing of the, the…" Penelope was stuttering and couldn't find the words to finish her sentence.

"It's okay," the other guard soothed, "we'll help you with this one." He bent down to one of the safety tanks on the floor and strained open the lock that secured the lid. The first guard then dipped a net in the main tank which contained the baby. After a few moments he hauled the net out of the water and squirming in it was the small emerald-tailed girl. He turned carefully towards the safety tank but suddenly Penelope found herself shouting something,

"Wait! Wait." She moved closer to the end of the pole where the net was, the small thing inside it was moving less now as she was drying out. Penelope began to put her hands into the net.

"Miss, what are you doing?" hissed one of the guards. Penelope hushed him and continued to entwine her fingers through the net. She had drawn the bracelet she had found beneath Lana's bed from her pocket and placed it gently round the child's neck. The shells rested heavy on her damp skin.

"Okay," Penelope swallowed, "you can take her now." The guard then slung the girl into the safety tank while the other quickly refastened the lid. They both looked at her with contempt and surprise as if she might be crazy. One of the guards tutted then said,

"I don't think you need our help, you can take her out from here." The two of them turned swiftly and left Penelope in the basement.

A small tank of water was heavy enough without a baby inside and Penelope couldn't even get a grip of it to lift it. She decided to slide it carefully with her feet across the basement floor. As she was pushing it nearer to the door, she noticed the fish-tailed girl was now regaining her energy. She was flipping and twirling and flitting about in the small confines of the tank. Penelope was mesmerised and bent down to have a look. As she did so, the little thing inside came crashing towards the edge of the tank so hard that the glass cracked slightly. Penelope yelped and jumped back. Suddenly she heard the clunk again as it smashed itself into the side once more. Penelope panicked. Was it trying to escape? Was it trying to get to Penelope? Quickly, Penelope flung open the basement door to the outside. It was only a few feet across mud before the edge of the river started. She got down and pushed the tank with two hands across the ground all the while the small fish-tailed girl repeatedly flinging herself at the glass. It was then that Penelope noticed her eyes. They were black, soulless. Her teeth were like a row of tiny shards of glass. Her skin looked as though it was melting. Penelope used the strength from her fear to give the tank one last push into the lake and as she did so the glass shattered and the baby disappeared into the water. Penelope leant back onto her elbows in the mud, breathing rapidly. What had she just seen? She tried to wrap her head around it. The girl had been so gentle in the big tank earlier, so tame. Now she had just tried to attack her. Her head felt muddled. She had tried for so long to convince both herself and Travis that these things weren't that bad but maybe he was right. Maybe she wasn't just trying to make Travis feel better by believing there was good in them. Maybe the reason she was able to sleep at night was because of this belief. After that attack though, Penelope wasn't sure if she would ever sleep again.

8

Arik and Kai had been summoned to the kitchen by their mother. They sat at the woodworm eaten table in an awkward silence opposite Vivienne. Arik decided to break the silence.

"What's going on, mum?" Before he hardly finished, Vivienne hastily responded,

"Just wait for your father please."

A few more minutes passed until their father skulked into the room and slumped in the remaining chair at the table. This wasn't Morgan's usual way of carrying himself, nor his normal posture for sitting in a chair. Arik thought he looked washed out and tired. He repeated his question but this time aimed it at his father.

"What's going on, Dad?"

"Well," Morgan gulped, "see the thing is, how do I say it… Your mum and I are having another baby." Kai jumped out of his seat.

"Wow! This is so great! Are you serious? I'm going to have a little brother or sister!" Kai began to run around the kitchen table singing something about being a big brother. Arik ignored him and stared at his parents. The forlorn looks in their eyes saddened him. They had told him stories before of the joy they had felt when they were expecting him. No such joy filled the air now. Instead tension and worry bounced between all three of them for Arik understood what this could potentially mean if the baby was to be a girl. He understood the dangers of giving birth out here on the stilt housing with no access to proper medical equipment or trained doctors. He even understood the difficulty of getting real nutrition with the measly rations his father brought back from The Mainland and the implications of this on pregnancy. For the first time in his life, Arik felt angry at his parents and maybe even disappointed. How could they be so foolish? His brother bumped into his chair.

"Watch it!" Arik snapped. "Stop dancing around like everything is okay! Stop pretending you don't know anything! God you're so childish Kai!" Arik slammed his chair into the floor and stormed off out of the room – out of the house. He had taken his anger out on Kai, the one person who didn't deserve it. While Arik stood outside and breathed in shaky gulps of sea air to try and calm himself, he could hear Kai sobbing from inside. He felt awful. He felt let down. He felt terrified. All these emotions burned inside him. He kept inhaling the cold air deeply to try and put out the fire that raged inside him. After about five minutes the door behind creaked open then clicked shut. It was Morgan.

"Son," he whispered in his soothing tone that Arik really appreciated at that moment, "look I'm sorry. Your mother and I, we're not overjoyed about the idea but we're not scared either. Remember that. For if we are not worried, you shouldn't be either. We are not your responsibility." Arik stared out at the flat black sea.

"No but the baby will be if it's, you know, a boy. I already have enough to deal with worrying about Kai." The thought of telling his dad then about Kai's 'special secret' of the Femaestus in the cove crossed Arik's mind but he could still faintly hear Kai sobbing inside. He'd already upset him enough tonight and couldn't bring himself to make it any worse.

"Kai isn't your responsibility either, Arik, but I know you look out and care for him and for that I am very grateful."

"And what if it's a girl? You just going to dump it in the sea with the rest of them?" Arik wasn't really taking in anything his father was saying but was venting his thoughts instead, "and what about Mum? What if anything happens to Mum? I don't want to lose Mum." Suddenly tears were rolling down Arik's bitter cold cheeks. He was taking in short sharp breaths and was unable to control his whimpering. Morgan pulled him into his warm chest.

"Come now," he said, "let's go back in to the warm. We shouldn't be out here at this time of night anyway." He ushered Arik back inside. Once they were through the door, Arik went straight over to his brother and pulled him in tight, just as his dad had done with him outside.

"Sorry for being mean, Kai" he whispered. He felt Kai's face muscles squeeze into a smile against his chest. Then, as he was holding his brother, he realised that his dad hadn't really answered any of his questions.

The next morning, Arik felt the need the make it up to his little brother. As soon as he awoke he turned to face Kai's bed which was a couple of feet away from his. "Psst! Kai, what do you want to do today," Arik smiled. Kai opened his gluey eyes and focused them on Arik. Then he rolled over.

"Nothing," he mumbled into his pillow.

"What do you mean nothing? Come on Kai, you're not still angry at me are you?"

"No," replied Kai, still with a mouthful of pillow, "just don't want to do anything today." Arik wasn't stupid. He had this natural instinct, like his dad, of just knowing things and he knew from Kai's tone that he had other plans for the day.

"So what do you have planned for today then?" he toyed. Kai shrugged his shoulders. It was the shoulder shrug that confirmed it for Arik that Kai had not kept his promise. "You're going to spy on that thing you think is your girlfriend, aren't you?" Kai flipped back over to face Arik and sat bolt upright.

"Piss off, Arik!" he spat and ran out of the bedroom. Arik's jaw gaped open. Did his little brother just curse at him? Where had he even learned such language? Arik realised that this 'special secret' must mean more to Kai than he had first thought. He had never seen such anger screwed up in his brother's sleepy face. Was Kai in too deep now with this Femaestus? Arik finally decided that he would tell his dad all about it when he returned from The Mainland later that day. It was for Kai's own good. Until then, Arik would spend the day not letting Kai out of his sight. It was chore day so there was no chance of Kai escaping before dad came home. Arik and Kai had a set of chores each to match their age and capabilities that their mum had set out for them. The first on Arik's list was emptying the toilet bowl into the sea while Kai's was to put things in their rightful places, such as books back on the bookshelf. They happily took up their jobs to the beautiful sound of their mum singing all the while.

By the time Arik was halfway down his list, he was also halfway up the chimney. Most of his jobs were the dirty ones but it was important that they kept it clean as the fireplace was their only source of heat. He wasn't sure how long he'd been up their when he remembered about keeping an eye on Kai. "Kai!" he yelled, "Kai!" No response. He decided to try his mother. "Mum!" he shouted, even louder this time, but she didn't reply either. He could faintly hear her singing and guessed she couldn't hear him over the sound of herself – but what was Kai's excuse? He could only be wiping the table or something which was well within earshot of the fireplace - unless he wasn't doing his chores. "Shit," Arik muttered under his breath as he began to scramble back down the chimney. He knew exactly where Kai was and he wasn't happy. Arik wormed his way out the fireplace and ran to the door, leaving black smuts in his path. He barged through the front door and started to make his way round the deck that lined the edge of the house when he heard a scream. "KAI!" he cried. He picked up speed and ran to the back of the deck. Flapping about on the deck was a thick armoured tail. It slammed into the deck, making it quiver beneath Arik's feet. The tail was quickly turning from a green that was almost black to a vivid shiny lime colour as the air dried it up. The skin on the body attached to it was tightening as it dried and the contours of the arms and ribs were softening. It was lying on its front, its arms reaching out to Kai who was lying on his back on the deck as if he'd fallen backwards. Suddenly the tail slammed into the deck again with a thud as if it was made out of solid rubber. The whole deck shuddered and rattled and caused Morgan's tool rack to fall from the side of the house. Arik knew he had to do something. He threw himself to the floor and began sifting through the rusty metal tools as quickly as he could until his hand felt the start of pole. Arik followed it with his eyes until the end where he realised it was a spear. He dragged it up with him, the metal scraping against the wooden deck. The sound alerted the Femaestus and she craned her neck to face Arik. Good. At least her attention was no longer on Kai. Arik took a few strides towards the giant flapping beast, double checked his grip and raised the spear above his head. As he did so, warm music flooded his ears. A voice so tender crawled up his spine and caused his arms to go weak. He paused. As he looked down at the beautiful monster he could see it was her singing to him. His arms began to wobble and soften and his heart was melting beyond his control. Kai's voice calmly interrupted the song,

'See Arik, see how beautiful she is. Don't do it.' Arik could tell from his soft jelly voice that the song was having the same effect on Kai. That's when he remembered it was a trap. 'This thing is dangerous' he reminded himself. He shook his head, held his breath and battled the song that invaded his ears to find strength. Then somehow, before he even hardly knew it, he slid the spear in between the Femaestus' shoulder bones. Thick crimson blood oozed out as two screams penetrated the air; the fish-tailed girls horrifying painful screech and Kai's desperate mournful one. It sounded like Kai screamed 'no' but it was a blurry mess to Arik as he watched the life leave the half-girl on the deck, her tail slowing from incredible convulsions to gentle taps. The pinky colour of her skin seemed to drain out with the blood and her green tail faded of all its lustre like a dead coral reef. She was no longer moving, no longer breathing. A corpse lay still in front of Arik and Kai.

"What have you done?" Kai whimpered, his eyes brimming with tears.

"Saved your life." Arik's pride and bravery smothered the sadness he would have otherwise felt for his brother. Kai burst into a flood of hysterical crying. He was mumbling through his tears something about how the thing wouldn't have hurt him and how he had just wanted to talk to her but Arik wasn't interested. He looked down at where the spear entered her back, slightly left of her spine. Arik had gotten her good. Then he noticed something wrapped around her thin wrist that was crumpled up by her face. He moved the spear slightly to push her hair aside to reveal a bracelet made of tiny little shells. It was then that Arik felt guilty. There was something so human about crafting a bracelet and decorating yourself with it that he felt murderous. He didn't feel in that moment like he had slain a monster but instead like he had stabbed a helpless human in the back like some coward. He could still hear Kai sobbing - then the sound of his mother coming around the deck calling their names. There was nothing they could do to hide what had happened. She was going to find out. Vivienne walked around the corner and screamed a short sharp scream before clasping her hands over her mouth.

"Get inside. Now!"

9

Penelope took the long route back through the hospital from the basement back to the lab. She needed some time to clear her mind and the lengthy corridors she had to walk and the stairs she needed to climb would give her plenty of time to do that. Guilt hung over her like a dark cloud. It was heavy and suppressing and she tried her best to think about anything else to shift it but it was useless. All she could think was back to the time when she and Travis first thought they had found a solution to everything. She replayed the story in her head. She remembered everything as though it was yesterday but this was a year ago now. As she ambled back through the hospital, she began to recall how one morning, just like any other day, she got into work and sipped the last dregs of her still-smouldering coffee before disposing of her cardboard cup and entering the lab. As soon as she opened the big lab door, Travis sprung up in her face with a childish bounce in his step and a glow she'd never seen before beaming from his face.

"I've had an idea! No wait. I've had *the* idea. The solution. Penelope oh it's great! Sit down, sit down!" Penelope hadn't even had a chance to remove her coat and Travis was already ushering her into a seat and blabbering words of enthusiasm from beneath his little white moustache that twitched eagerly when he was excited. "Penelope, listen to me. The rising sea levels, the threat of the oceans covering our land, I've stumbled across the perfect solution! We all know stilt housing won't be enough, people will still die, well I have found a way in which everybody will live! We don't fight it Penelope, we *join* it." Penelope wasn't sure if she liked where Travis was going with this, but something about his bubbliness made her keen to hear what was next. Travis suddenly yanked

Penelope out of her seat and dragged her to the back of the lab. "Come!"

By the window at the back was a small clear plastic box that Travis was pointing and smiling at. Penelope peered closer. A tiny rat was hunched over inside it, nibbling on something. At first, Penelope saw nothing noticeable about this rat, other than that it was in a box, not a cage like the other rats. Before Penelope knew it, Travis began filling the tub with water.

"What are you doing, Travis? You'll drown it!"

"Wait! Watch." Travis was grinning as he poured the water three times as deep as the height of the rat. Soon it was completely submerged. Then that's when Penelope saw it.

"It's breathing. You've given it gills!" Travis let out a yelp of excitement. "So this is your plan, Travis?"

"That's right, Penelope. We'll use this epigenetic vaccine which I have created to develop gills and every other necessity for us to live under the water when it comes."

"Travis, this is brilliant. Although, I'm not sure everyone will want to live under the water but it's brilliant that you've developed the option to do so!"

"I know. Now all I have to do is test it on a human to check it works. It takes a couple of weeks for the gills to develop on the rats following injection and I anticipate it will be about the same for humans." Travis was almost breathless with excitement. Penelope adored his enthusiasm, his brain power and loved working with Travis. She knew it was her duty to offer herself up as first volunteer and she almost said it immediately but first asked,

"What's in it? How did you do it?"

"Oh, Penelope there is so much in it. It's taken me years of messing with proteins and DNA and all that. I've been trying desperately to create an injection that manipulates our DNA in order to create a heritable phenotypic change in humans – in this case gills - but the main ingredient that set it off was the stem cells from an axolotl; it was only once I added these that the gel became active and I just knew then, before even testing on the rats, that something was going to work. I then started injecting them and of course there were a few mishaps at first but I've tweaked it to perfection now and you know with the axolotls ability to regrow limbs who knows what else we may end up capable of and-"

"Okay, Travis, this is incredible." Penelope had heard enough of Travis' rambling. He was so overexcited by this point he was just talking incessantly at her and, besides, she didn't really care at that moment what was in it, she just wanted to find out sooner rather than later if it would work. If Travis had really found a solution to the impending water level rise, she wanted to be part of that discovery. She cleared her throat hastily before Travis had a chance to start up again.

"We need to find a test subject; we need to find a *human* test subject," she explained. Travis' mouth wrangled into an awkward twist as if he'd already thought this through.

"It has to be one of us," he gulped, "this can't get out to anyone until we know for certain that it works. There will be chaos on the streets if word gets out about a potential solution, people will riot and fight to be first in line if it means their chances of drowning in the future is diminished. Then what if it doesn't work after that? No, we can't trust anyone else with this yet. It has to be one of us." Travis repeated the last bit with grave sincerity in his voice. Penelope understood. Silence sat between them causing the anxiety in each of them to rise to uncomfortable levels.

"I should do it." Travis finally exhaled the words heavily as if he'd being holding his breath since he last spoke. Suddenly Penelope felt a change in her too.

"No, it should be me," she sighed, "you're the brains, Travis. What if something went...wrong? The world can't lose you."

"And I can't lose you!" he jumped in.

"Travis, the world is bigger than me and right now the world needs this." Travis swirled his finger around in the tub of water the rat was still happily bouncing around in. Penelope could see in his scrunched-up face that he was thinking, pondering hard. He needed more convincing.

"Please, Travis, I *want* to do this. Please let me." Penelope placed a hand on his arm and he gazed up at her with wide worried eyes.

"Are you sure?"

"Yes, Travis, I'm sure." Penelope felt in that moment that she was actually more eager than Travis. Travis said no more words for he knew there was no swaying his headstrong assistant once she had her mind set on something. He wiped a small square on her arm with a light, cold, sterile anaesthetic on a cotton swab then turned to get the needle from the cooler. Suddenly Travis felt scared. His hands shook violently as he squeezed excess air from the syringe. He thought about asking Penelope again if she was sure but as he looked down at her all he could see in her face was bravery and determination sat unwavering in her eyes. Why did he feel doubt overcome him all of a sudden, if Penelope was fine? Did she have more faith in him than he did himself? He inhaled slowly and exhaled even slower to try and calm his shaky hands. He had to do this. He leant in towards Penelope and slowly pushed the silver point into her skin. It was thick and tough and the syringe was heavy to push such a thick vaccine into her body. Penelope's face began to screw up and she started to whimper slightly. Travis noticed but continued pushing.

"Just a bit more," he uttered through gritted teeth. He was using up a lot of strength forcing the sludge into Penelope's arm. Penelope was burning up. Her face turned almost mauve and she stopped breathing for the last bit until finally Travis shouted, "Done!" and he whipped the needle out of her arm. Penelope immediately flung her arm away but accidentally smashed it against the lab worktop and shattered two conical flasks. Shards of glass penetrated the underneath of her arm and severed her skin deep.

"Ouch!!" Penelope yelped.

"Okay, okay, calm down, calm down," Travis soothed. "Jesus, that was some injection huh?"

"Some injection? I just tore my arm up Travis!" Penelope's arm throbbed from both the injection and from cutting it open. Travis helped her off the chair and she hobbled over to the big stainless steel sink and began running the warm taps. She placed her bleeding arm under the running water and let it soothe her skin and cuts. The blood made a creamy pinkish swirl down the plug hole. She watched it run down as she took deep breaths trying to calm herself.

"I'm sorry about your arm Penelope, I didn't realise it was going to be so painful."

"It's okay Travis, but if this works, maybe we should work on finding an easier way of administering it before we release it on the public. It definitely needs a bit more work doing on it…"

It was at the recollection of that moment, when Penelope remembered suggesting they do more work on the vaccine, that she had reached the lab after navigating her way back through the hospital from the basement. She had been so much more focused on her thoughts than where she was actually going that she had completely lost track of how long she had been gone. She stopped, sighed and stared intently at the heavy silver door. She knew in her heart that Travis and herself needed to have a serious conversation about what happened that day and get it off their chests. They had to admit, out in the open, what happened when they first tried out the vaccine. They had to admit that it had entered the water supply and that was what had mutated everybody's DNA – the result of which was that all the baby girls were being born as Femaestus. Neither of them had ever mentioned it to each other despite the fact girls had been born with tails since then – yet it was clear to her that they both knew what the truth was deep down and now was the time to face it. For it was this weight that prevented Travis sleeping and caused him to age exponentially and Penelope wanted desperately to help her mentor. She decided she would be upfront as soon as she walked into the lab. She took a deep breath in, pushed the door open and peered into the room. It was empty. Travis was nowhere to be seen. Penelope called out but there was no response. She calmly waltzed round the room, checking behind the counters and cupboards. He was gone and Penelope began to feel uneasy as though something wasn't right. She picked up pace and scampered out into the corridor. She called Travis' name again but the corridor was empty in both directions. Penelope squinted her eyes. A small square of daylight illuminated the cold tile floor at the far end of the right corridor. The fire exit door was open. Penelope scarpered down the hall all the way to the end where a slight breeze met her flustered face.

"Travis!" She yelled out into the open sea air. The slate grey feeling of worry that had previously sat in her stomach now grew into dread.

"Travis!" she screamed again as she stumbled outside and clambered over the jagged rocks that lined the cliff edge. But before she even made it to the very edge, she spotted the familiar sight of Travis' small metal spectacles laying bent up between two rocks ahead of her. Carefully, she dragged herself across a few more rocks to reach them. She picked them up shakily then stared out at the sea. Her hair whipped her face gently as the sun slowly burnt her skin. The sea below was choppy and rocky and a bed of death.

Penelope sunk her face into her hands and sobbed heavy heartedly into her palms.

10

The sky was black outside as Vivienne stared blankly into the shabby dressing table mirror, her room illuminated only slightly by a small oil lamp. The mirror reminded her of the one she used to have back on The Mainland. Both had the same ornate metal lacing the edges and embracing the big oval shape glass in the middle. Except hers had been pristine. It was always polished and buffed and beautiful. This one she had in front of her now was turning jade at the ridges of the metal as if encrusted with dying barnacles. Perhaps they were barnacles, after all Morgan had fished it out of the edge of the water for her on his way back from The Mainland one day. It was supposed to bring her happiness but every time she looked into it she was just reminded of the life they had before. Then she noticed something else different – her reflection. The last time she had looked in her mirror on the Mainland she had also been pregnant. She recalled her face glowing a soulful bronze hue and her blue eyes sparkling like the ocean water. She remembered her bouncy chestnut hair enveloping her face and shoulders and her plump skin being as soft as a new-borns blanket. Now Vivienne looked in the mirror and saw nothing but a crumbling grey woman with dry tired eyes and tormented skin. She placed her hand on her stomach. She knew it was full of life but it felt empty. How could she be so selfish? Panic suddenly flooded her bloodstream. It's not like she hadn't already thought about the consequences of this baby being a girl but in that moment, gazing at her reflection and holding her belly, her heart filled with fear. Partly because of the thought of the entire pregnancy and birth process out on the stilt housing but also because she started to think about Mercia.

Mercia was Vivienne's best friend back on The Mainland. She was there through her pregnancy with Arik and even attended the birth. Vivienne always saw them both more as sisters. After Arik was born, Mercia was always around helping Vivienne whenever Morgan was at work and playing a big part in Arik's first years.

"It's making me so broody, Vivienne!" Mercia would beam. Vivienne knew that Mercia and her boyfriend, Joe, had been trying for some time now for a baby but she never expressed any sadness or jealousy. Vivienne admired Mercia's strength and positivity and always prayed that she would too be blessed with a child.

A couple of years later Mercia announced her long overdue pregnancy. She was elated and so was Vivienne. Now it was Vivienne's turn to be a shoulder of support to her best friend, not that she was needed much because Mercia was so strong and independent. However Mercia still made it clear how much she wanted Vivienne to be a part of her child's entrance into the world. One day, on the way to the hospital for the 20-week scan to find out the sex, Mercia turned to Vivienne and said, "I want you to be at the birth, just like I was for Arik's." Vivienne wept with joy and embraced her best friend and kissed her tiny stomach as they entered the hospital.

"Of course," sobbed Vivienne, "no matter what, I'll be there."

Mercia laid on the hard hospital bed and lifted her top. Cold gloopy gel was squeezed onto her tummy as the doctor pressed the ultrasound scanner into her. Vivienne wasn't looking at Mercia or the doctor but instead was grinning eagerly at the screen. The doctor moved the curved stick around and around. He traced bumps and lines round her stomach and pushed in and pulled out regularly. There was silence for what seemed like an age and Mercia started to feel a little uneasy until eventually the doctor cleared his throat and said,

"I'm not entirely sure why but I cannot seem to get a picture of the bottom half of your baby my dear. I've woken your little one and made them wriggle around for me to get a better view but I just still cannot see anything. It looks as though you will have to come back in a month's time after further development. Maybe when he or she is a bit bigger I will be able to see something." The doctor's voice was wobbly and cracked. Vivienne wasn't sure she trusted what he was saying and Mercia's uneasiness broke out into full panic once they left the room.

"What's going on? What's wrong with my baby? Why can't they determine the sex?" She blasted Vivienne with unanswerable questions.

"Hush, hush," cooed Vivienne as she held her friend in close to her, "don't worry. There's nothing to worry about. Sometimes these things happen. Look, in a month's time you'll know whether that's a little boy or girl you've got brewing in there and everything will be ok." Vivienne wrenched her face into the best smile she could manage without it looking false.

Less than one month later, Vivienne was startled by a shrill sound in the middle of the night. At first, in her misty sleepiness she assumed it was Arik waking up – then she became aware that it was in fact the phone ringing.

"Hello?"

"Viv, it's Joe, it's Mercia, she's been rushed into the hospital. She woke up screaming. She was bleeding. There was blood everywhere. She was screaming. She was screaming so much. Viv she screamed for you. Viv she *needs* you. Hurry up Viv hurr-"

"I'm on my way." Vivienne hung up the phone and shook Morgan gently. "I have to go up the hospital, it's Mercia, something isn't right." Morgan rubbed his eyes and gently whispered to his wife "go."

Vivienne hurled through the doors of the hospital and ran up to reception.

"Mercia, Mercia Day, she's just been rushed in where can I find her?" The receptionist explained where Vivienne could find her best friend, her sister, and so Vivienne shot through the hospital as fast as she could. As she half ran, half walked up the final corridor, blood-curdling screams began to ricochet off the walls.

"Mercia…" Vivienne's face turned white as she followed the sounds of the screams. Finally she came to two double doors with small rectangle windows. The doors were locked. Vivienne slammed them with both hands and howled.

"LET ME IN!" she cried but her voice was silenced by Mercia's wailing. Of the five or six doctors in the room, not one looked up. Vivienne scraped and banged and screeched but nobody was coming to let her in. She looked through one of the small windows and could see Mercia's back arching. Her eyes followed up her body to her neck where thick veins were protruding from her skin. Her face was so dark mauve like a deep plum colour and the expression on her face could only be described as agony and torture. Having gone through labour herself, Vivienne knew full well how painful it was - but this wasn't right; besides it was far too early in the pregnancy for Mercia to be giving birth now anyway. She looked through the other window, all the while Mercia's screaming growing darker like an ink black puddle saturating the air. What Vivienne didn't know then was that what she was about to see when she looked through the other window would never leave her mind. One of the doctors had two gloved hands stuck in Mercia's stomach and was just starting to remove them. As his hands pulled out, Vivienne saw the tiniest, translucent head and delicate shoulders, followed by bloody arms smaller than the doctor's fingers. Then she saw the fragile chest and small stomach and then... And then nothing. Dangling above Mercia's torn open stomach was just half of a lifeless foetus with underdeveloped skin just about holding it's intestines inside it. Vivienne gasped. The screaming stopped. Silence. Two doctors lay the half baby on some hospital towel on the side while two others checked Mercia for signs of life. Vivienne saw the one with his fingers on her pulse shake his head.

"NO!" wailed Vivienne. "NO! No! What happened! What *happened?!"* she cried as she slid down to the floor with her back against the doors.

Vivienne shook her head and looked back into the mirror. Mercia must have been one of the first people to miscarry a Femaestus and it killed her. And that was in a hospital surrounded by trained medical staff and proper equipment. Not that anybody really knew back then what was happening – Vivienne certainly didn't. All they knew was that they had to get that baby out before it killed Mercia, there was no time for anaesthetics or epidurals, but it took her life regardless. The horror of that night never stopped replaying in Vivienne's mind. It would creep into her day dreams and stalk through her nightmares. Now that horror physically sat in the pit of her womb. Being three months into pregnancy meant she could still miscarry. How much longer did she have left to live? She could miscarry at any second. She could go full term but die giving birth. She could have a baby boy and it could all go smoothly. She pictured the veins that bulged from Mercia's neck. She recalled the screams that rattled the hospital walls. She remembered the half baby suspended in the air. She thought about Mercia's lifeless body. She imagined leaving her sons alone in this world. With that, she threw her fist into the oval glass of the mirror, ripped it off its hinges and slung it out the nearest window. It slid across the deck and teetered for a brief second on the edge before falling to the depths below, shattered and broken.

All the while, Arik had been crouched on the deck out in the black night air with his back against the house, running the bracelet, which he had taken off the Femaestus, between his fingers over and over again. Kai was in bed. His mum was in some state of shock in her bedroom. Arik was waiting for his dad to return from The Mainland. He knew he shouldn't be outside, especially not alone in the dark but nobody was stopping him, plus, he now felt like he could handle himself should any danger emerge. He needed to be outside, to breathe, to think. How was his dad going to react to Kai's infatuation with a monster, to Arik's murderous actions but most of all how was he going to react to his pregnant wife being in an inconsolable state of shock? Arik could smell the Femaestus. She was round the corner toward the back of the deck lying unmoved from the spot where he had taken her life. She smelled fishy. She smelled as though she was decaying faster than any human body. A whiff of the pungent stench suffocated the air every now and again and made Arik sick to his stomach. "Horrible fishy monsters," Arik muttered to himself under his breath as he toyed with the shells on the bracelet. Suddenly the silence was broken by a smashing of glass and his mum's mirror came flying out the window.

"Mum?! Are you okay?" Arik grabbed the ledge and peered in to see his mum just sitting there, turned slightly away from him, blood on her hands. "Mum?"

"Go away, Arik"

"But mum, your hand-"

"I said go! It's nothing."

Arik backed away from the window, silently. Then he heard a splash. He turned to see that the mirror, which had been wavering on the edge of the deck, had finally tipped over and plummeted into the sea. Arik couldn't let that sink; he knew his mum loved it really. He ran to the edge and dived forward thrusting his hand in the water to try and grab it but he slipped on the deck and slid beneath the bottom fence pole and followed the mirror straight into the water. Arik gasped on the way in but still managed to gulp half a mouthful of water. He began kicking and waving frantically – could he swim? Of course he couldn't he had never been in the water! Panic engulfed him as he was sinking further down into the blackness. He looked up but the faint light where the moonlight hit the surface was already so far away. Around him tiny shards of the glass glittered and danced about him. They strangely calmed him slightly. He battled his body's urge to breathe and kept kicking but it was no use. His head was going dizzy and his lungs were aching for a breath. Then, in the distance further down below him, a faint light began glowing. It burned bigger and brighter as it approached him, it's light cerulean hue cutting through the blackness. He was about to try and breathe – he could feel it. Just before he inhaled lungful of water, he glimpsed the monstrous face of a deadly woman, with grey skin like grated seaweed, emerge from the glow. Her jaw seemed enlarged like it was housing rows of deadly teeth. Through gaping holes in her skin Arik could make out bone. He felt her deathly cold hands clasp his face. Fear flashed straight through to his core. Then he breathed in and blacked out.

11

Following Travis' suicide, and her encounter with the baby Femaestus in the basement, Penelope decided she could no longer continue with her job at the hospital. She knew however that she had to give good reason and find a decent place to move on to that could give evidence that she was continuing to provide support and research for the future of humanity. Otherwise her place on The Mainland would be lost. One day, she arranged to meet with the board of governors at the Town Hall in the very centre of The Mainland. It was only a short walk from the hospital so she had arranged for her appointment to be during her lunch break. The Town Hall was where everybody on The Mainland went for all sorts of queries, issues and requests. Penelope's request was for a job. Things didn't work in the same way now as they had in the old days. You didn't go for an interview or send off applications. You had to go to the Town Hall and be assigned by the people in charge of The Mainland. When Penelope arrived at the Town Hall she entered through two ornate brown doors that had a cliché lion's head knocker on each. Through the doors was simply just an open hall with an elevated desk at one end behind which sat four stern looking men. Penelope straightened her posture and marched up to them looking as keen and brave as she possibly could. She cleared her throat and introduced herself but the men did not respond, they simply stared at her. She began to feel awkward and so continued with her request. She asked for a job where she could utilise her knowledge of science and where her participation in the research for a cure for the Femaestus could be useful. She told them that she wanted to spend 'less time throwing them away and more time working closely with people to help find a cure'. The board liked this although it wasn't the truth. Penelope couldn't bear to dispose of another new-born baby or work in any death lab. The part about finding a cure was the truth though. She had to even more so now, in Travis' memory. After an inaudible discussion among the board, the chairman finally rose and told Penelope that she would from now on work at S.T.A.B. in the heart of The Mainland where all the 'real' tests were going on. Penelope didn't know what he meant by 'real' tests. Nor did she know that S.T.A.B. stood for *Study of The Adult Body*. All she knew was she would be glad to be rid of that hospital and the baby disposal unit.

However, if Penelope had known then what S.T.A.B. was going to be like, maybe she would've remained at the hospital.

At first S.T.A.B. had a kind vibe to it. Penelope thought it seemed more like a hospice. There were a lot of ill adults lying around on beds, not talking or moving, just slightly moaning now and again. Penelope thought these must be cancer patients or people with some other form of terminal illness without much hope left who have come here for one final chance at life. On her first day she was paired with a lady called Grace. Grace had been working at S.T.A.B. for many years and Penelope felt grateful that she had been paired with someone with such experience. Grace was kind and clever but also well-grounded and strong.

"Most of the work being done at S.T.A.B. is experimental and while this sometimes yields great results, other times it has some not so pleasant effects," explained Grace as she toured Penelope through the building, "but what we are trying to achieve here is for the good of the future of mankind and as you know, that's the most important goal in all our lives right now." Penelope nodded fast like an obedient dog as she shuffled along behind Grace. The halls and rooms did not look or feel as they had back at hospital. They were painted in smooth dark oranges and teals with solid black silhouettes of trees and patterns curving up the walls. The floor was dark wide wooden planks, not white shiny linoleum like the floors of the hospital. It wasn't busy and rushed. It was calm. Then

Penelope realised that that's because they had only passed one other doctor since touring the whole building, the only other people in there were patients.

"Where's all the staff? How does such a little number of staff handle so many patients?"

"We don't need many staff. Most of the patients are kept heavily sedated due to the fact we are unsure of what painful side effects our experiments may have on them. They don't cause us any trouble that way." Penelope was sure Grace winked at her at the end of that sentence. Surely not. Penelope shook her head. "Right," Grace continued, "if you want to make yourself at home in here for a bit, I'll be back soon with a list of tasks you can get on with today, you'll mainly be helping me with bits, ok?"

"Sure." Penelope watched Grace glide out into the corridor and listened to her footsteps get quieter and quieter as she moved away down the silent hall. Penelope looked around. She was in an open room that looked like an obsolete canteen. The old food shelves and serving desk and queuing area was there but there were no trays, no plates, no food, no seats, no tables and no people. Penelope sat alone on a single chair in the room. Five minutes passed and she was getting restless and so decided that wandering into the next room could do no harm. As she approached the open doorway of the next room she could see it was some kind of ward. Eight gaunt men lay straight in their beds staring up at the ceiling, a big TV playing on a very low murmuring volume in the corner. It seemed so sad and boring. Penelope sidled up to one of the men in their bed. He looked like he needed a friendly face and a chat to cheer him up so that's what she was going to provide for him. As she got nearer, the man started to moan slightly. Then his breathing picked up. His chest began rising and falling rapidly. His moans were getting louder. Soon Penelope was standing over him and his eyes began darting left and right with alarming speed.

"Please, shhh," hushed Penelope, "it's okay I've just come over for a chat." She placed her hand gently on his torso and his chest bolted. It was as if he had tried to jump away from her but couldn't move.

"Please, talk to me, are you okay?" as she said this, the man began to open his mouth, then a firm hand grabbed her by the shoulder. As she was spun round she caught a final glimpse of the man's mouth and she could have sworn it was sewed shut with what looked like black plastic cable ties.

"What are you doing in here!?" Exclaimed Grace, "I told you to wait in the other room." She began dragging Penelope out of the room via a firm grip on her arm.

"That man, Grace, we have to help him, his mouth, it's sewed up!"

Graced sighed and slumped her head forward so her black straight hair hung loosely in front of her glasses. "I know."

"What?!"

"I know that man's mouth is sewed up, Penelope."

"Well why?! What sort of place *is* this?" Penelope was stuttering and shaking and breathing hard.

"Remember the first thing I said to you when you came in about some results not being quite as pleasant? You told me you understood. Clearly you don't. That man in there had a severe reaction to an experimental cure we used on him. He had terminal throat cancer. We used one of our experiments on him and unfortunately it did not work. He still has the cancer but also in addition to that now he has to have his mouth sewed up. If he doesn't, he will eat himself to death. The particular cure we tried on that man produced cannibalistic effects on a number of patients. We've had to go back to the drawing board on that one." Grace's voice was fading, possibly even whimpering. Penelope felt her sadness permeate the air and almost felt an urge to hold her.

"I'm, I'm sorry. I didn't realise-"

"Well maybe in future you don't make assumptions until you *do* realise." Grace flicked her head back and glared at Penelope before grabbing her pen and clipboard and standing up. "You can go home today. Think of today as an induction. I'll see you tomorrow." Penelope gulped as she turned and slunk out of the building, Grace watching her all the way.

12

Arik opened his eyes. His initial thought was that he was in his bed and was just waking up for another usual day. Then he felt a coolness embracing his lower half. It was water. Clear shiny aqua swirled around his waist. He went to stretch out his fingers to feel the smoothness of the water between them but he couldn't. His hands were tied. He shook them a couple of times but it was no use. They were tied behind his back and he was sat on a ledge in some kind of pool, another thicker rope pulled round his chest and under his arms securing him in place. The sandy rocks that made up the edge of the pool continued across the floor, up the walls and became the ceiling. Arik was in some kind of cave. Up high, directly above him, was a large opening which allowed daylight to flood the place. Arik could see the sky, the beautiful blue sky, full of air and open space. He took a deep breath in but rather than feel relaxed, he began to feel panic. It triggered memories of the last time he wanted desperately to take a deep breath in.

"Femaestus!" Arik found himself muttering out loud. He started to squirm and shift in his panic. He had to escape before it got back. But how was he still alive? Had he been saved - or even spared? There was no time to consider positive thoughts. Arik continued to flip his body about frantically like a fish on land and rattle his hands as much as possible but he was simply getting nowhere. Just as he was about to use his final bit of strength to perform one last shake he noticed a dark glow increasing in size below the opposite edge of the pool. He stopped dead still. He held his breath. He couldn't control his heartbeat though which was rapidly increasing in pace. He was sure the tremors would vibrate through his body and be detectable in the water but there was nothing he could do. He couldn't calm himself. The smudge beneath the water grew larger as it approached him. It began to near the surface and he was able to begin making out the now familiar shape of a woman's torso. Her hair was floating all around making undulating patterns in the water. Her thin arms reached forward slowly as her head surfaced. Out of the water, her hair became limp and stuck to her skin as if it had lost its life from leaving its comfort zone. Still it shined like new copper. She lifted her head and her beauty took Arik's breath away. Her large wide eyes glistened below a thick layer of dark wet eyelashes. Her pure pearl skin looked as though it would bruise if you so much as brushed a feather against it. Tiny droplets of water teetered on her partially parted lips. Arik wanted to taste those water droplets. He wanted to feel her hair and look deeper into her eyes. He suddenly became aware of his own gaping jaw and bulbous eyes and rattled his head in self-disdain.

"Stay away from me! What am I doing here? Stay back!" His attempt to sound brave and unperturbed by her presence was doused in fear as well as fascination. The Femaestus didn't respond. She smiled slightly before beginning to bob gradually closer to Arik. "I said stay back!" Arik repeated his command but to no avail.

"Hush," she whispered. She drew a long milky arm out of the water and cupped Arik's jaw gently. Then she tilted her head to the side slightly and smiled. "You are the land boy who watches?" Arik was confused. This couldn't be the Femaestus he and Kai had seen in the cove that day for he had slain that one on his deck. Hadn't he? He looked at the beauty in front of him. He acknowledged her copper hair and her blue waistline. Then he thought back to the one on the deck that day. She had had black hair and a bottle green tail. It wasn't her. "You are," she soothed. Arik suddenly felt awkward. He was no longer scared but was now having difficulty in finding words to say to this girl – *thing*. That's right. *It* was a *thing* and Arik was not going to let himself succumb to her. "Look, why am I here – why haven't you *eaten* me?"

"Where did you get this?" Suddenly her soft hold of his face became a tight clasp on his wrist as she began untying his hands. She dragged his hand roughly from behind his back and held the arm up that had the shell bracelet on it.

"I killed one of you and took this from it." Arik said this calmly without hesitation. He was smug as he felt like he had the control again.

"Do you know what it is?" Arik's face dropped along with the control he just thought he had. The thought of saying 'a bracelet' crossed his mind although he was smart enough to realise now that it was clearly more than just that and he felt far too grown up in this moment to say it anyway sarcastically.

"Tell me," he sighed.

"It's a bracelet. This bracelet has... a unique quality. When we are near the wearer of this bracelet we cannot attack – we do not want to attack. It helps take away our animalistic side. We see people as people – not as food. With this on you I see a person. I see you." Her voice cracked. Arik felt torn. He felt like he wanted to let his guard down – but how could he be sure this wasn't part of the trick of seduction? He stared into this girl's mournful eyes. If it wasn't true she would have eaten him by now. There had never been a known case of a Femaestus to hold back on dinner.

"You say you got it from one of us, tell me, did she attack you?" Arik went to immediately shout yes but then stopped and replayed the event with Kai and the Femaestus again in his mind, this time from a different perspective. Kai had been adamant that she wasn't going to hurt him but Arik had seen through his naivety. Also she had begun singing her siren song – this Arik knew for sure was a seduction technique from stories he had heard from his father. Plus she was up on the deck. What other reason would she have had to be up there than to have his little brother as a snack? But then Arik heard the question again in his mind, *"did she attack you?"* Arik hung his head and closed his eyes and whispered, "No."

When he actually thought about it, the Femaestus hadn't been attacking Kai and wasn't making any attempt to seduce or attack him until he came at her with a spear – naturally she was going to defend herself! He had taken her life and she was innocent. She had been wearing the bracelet. Arik's eyes began to well up.

"I'm sorry," he found himself utter. His head was still hanging low until the Femaestus' dainty fingers cupped his chin and tilted his face up towards hers.

"It is not your fault. We are misunderstood girls trapped under a curse we cannot break. It is said this bracelet is infused with the blood and love of a mother that once gave birth to a little girl whom was taken from her. It holds properties that could help end all this - but how, nobody knows." The girl's pupils dilated with sadness and Arik could see deep inside in that moment. He could see her soul. This girl had never met her mum. She had never met her father or any brothers she might have. Arik couldn't imagine life without his family. That's when he realised these girls needed help - not to be feared.

"I'm going to help you. All of you. I'm going to take the bracelet to The Mainland and let others know about it and get everything back the way it once was."

"You would do that?"

"Yes." As the golden sunlight poured down through the cave opening and splashed on the girls face, illuminating it's true beauty, Arik asked, "What is your name?"

"Tempestas," she replied in her sweet syrup voice.

"Such a beautiful name..." he accidentally responded out loud. He cleared his throat immediately upon realisation. "Tempestas, I'm Arik. Now, free me from these chains so I can get back home and tell my father everything and begin our journey to The Mainland." Tempestas began to untie him with a wry smile on her face. "What are you smiling for?"

"It's a fair way back through the waters to your home; you'll have to hold on to me close."

Arik felt the corners of his mouth curl up into an untameable smile, "that's fine with me," he whispered heavily into her ear.

"There's just one thing I ask before we leave this cave," Tempestas added, her voice suddenly laden with mysterious sadness. "Please, any time we have to swim beneath the surface, keep your eyes closed."

Arik thought about her request and knew why she had asked of it. He knew that the second she was below the surface her beauty would be diminished, the true soul of a Femaestus laid bare on the exterior of her body. He knew she'd be terrifying below the surface and gladly agreed to respect her request.

"Of course," he soothed as he wrapped his hands around her petite waist, "now let's go."

■■■

13

Penelope ambled slowly along the path leading up to the big off-white S.T.A.B. building. The outside was encased in grey metal girders and the overlaying dull cream metal beneath looked as though a giant hole punch had eaten its way through it where the sheets joined. She hadn't really realised before how foreboding the building truly was from the outside. The slim rectangle glass doors, which were guarded either side by two sad artificial potted trees, slid open silently as she approached them. Penelope thought about the day she had waiting ahead of her. She had been at S.T.A.B. for about a year now and each day was just like the last; feeding sick people with unknown illnesses, ensuring people remained hooked up to their drips, changing vile bedpans and sheets, sponging the skin of the sick and frequently being checked up on under the watchful eye of Grace. Penelope had been assigned to the East Wing of the clinic and was in charge of looking after the people on all four wards of that wing. Although Penelope was starting to think the word 'assigned' was not the correct term at all. Every time she almost wandered into a different room or strayed a little too far down a corridor that was off limits, Grace would appear out of nowhere, swishing her shiny black hair against her equally as shiny glasses. She would start tutting and asking what use Penelope could possibly have to be wherever she was. Penelope always apologised and told her she had gotten lost or confused. 'Assigned' was definitely not the right term - more like 'restricted.'

As Penelope stepped into the foyer, she immediately spotted Grace in her usual all black, tight fitting attire. She was talking to a man Penelope had never seen before. He was a tall man, with thin fair hair and a kind face and was dressed in casual khaki. He was nodding and smiling and Penelope felt a little mesmerised. She decided to walk past Grace to say good morning in the hope to get an introduction but Grace caught her approaching and quickly ushered the gentleman away down an 'off limit' corridor. Penelope sighed and bout turned towards the direction of her ward. She had gotten her hopes up too high just then that today might be slightly different to any other day.

Midday gradually came around and Penelope had been getting on with her usual tasks when it suddenly occurred to her that Grace had not bothered her all morning. Four or five times by now she would usually have been spied on by the darkly dressed damsel but Penelope hadn't noticed her once. Once Penelope had fed and watered all the patients and there had still been no sign of Grace she decided to go and look for her - not that she actually wanted to find her but that she just wanted to get out of the East Wing for a while and since Grace seemed to be otherwise preoccupied she figured she may as well. But looking for Grace would be her reason for 'wandering' should she get stopped. A few familiar corridors later, Penelope found herself in part of the building she had never been before. The walls here were a dry mustard yellow with crumbling damp patches and the floors were more hospital-like. The essence of warmth was lost down here and Penelope felt chills crawl down her chest. It was deathly quiet. Maybe this part of the building was obsolete and there was nothing down here, hence the dilapidation and neglect. Still, Penelope was intrigued and continued further. Her dainty footsteps seemed huge in the silence and she began to feel a sense of loneliness. She had been walking for about five minutes and had turned the corners of multiple corridors and passed dozens of empty or locked rooms. There was nothing down here. Penelope sighed. What had she been hoping for anyway? Something, just anything, to lift her mundane routine from its normality. Then, just as this thought lingered in her mind, she heard a startling cry - almost a scream, but it sounded restricted - coming from the opposite end of the corridor she was down. Penelope flung herself round to face the direction of where the noise came from. Again, it rang out, but this time it sounded as though it was cut short. Penelope began taking small steps down the corridor then faster and faster ones until she was almost at a jogging pace. She was breathing heavily as she got closer. Someone must be trapped, or in trouble! Her panicky thoughts motivated her legs to move faster. Just as she was approaching the end of the corridor she began to slow and the cry ricocheted off the walls once more, this time louder and more blood-curdling. "Hello!!" She yelled out, trying to determine which room the sound was coming from. Then she noticed a slight crack in one of the doors, it had been left ajar. She hastened towards the door and flung it open. Her heart dropped into her gut and the blood drained from her head. Vomit rose in her throat and filled her mouth. The stench was rotten but the sight was so much worse. In front of her was a dentist type chair, saturated with blood and basking in a thick clotting puddle of even more blood. On the chair was the man from the foyer earlier that day. His eyes were wide with terror and black tape was stuck across his lips. His hands were chained down and his legs... his legs were gone.

The sick that filled Penelope's mouth released and she threw up twice before she could even begin talking to the victim on the chair. She untied her little white half apron and clasped it over her mouth and nose before rushing over to the man and pulling off his tape.

"What happened to you?" Penelope asked in a desperate cry. The man was sweating profusely and shaking in a way only a trauma would make a person shake.

"Th, th, there-" he pushed out a word and with all his remaining strength nodded his burning head towards the side of the room. Penelope spun round to see three huge cylinders made of chunky glass and filled with water. Bubbles were rising up inside as if to keep the water oxygenated but every now and again the bubbles cleared and Penelope saw what was inside. In each tube a striking, solid, scaly tail. Penelope gasped. She wanted to ask the man more questions but there was no time. She began fumbling with the chains around his hands but as she did so she heard a clang from outside in the corridor. Penelope dropped the chains

"No, no, don't leave me," the man whimpered.

"Shhhh!" hushed Penelope, "I am not going to leave you." Footsteps became apparent somewhere down the corridor and Penelope knew she didn't have much time. She scouted the room, darting her eyes around rapidly for somewhere to hide. A rickety old desk was pushed up close to the wall in the corner. Penelope made a dash for it but as she arrived at the desk she realised she'd left bloody footprints in her wake - she had left a path to her hiding place. She jumped back out and began wiping them with her half-apron but it was no use. It was saturated and the blood just kept smearing. The footsteps were gaining on her and voices could now be heard but only murmuring - nothing distinct. When she looked around, and found nothing else with which to wipe the bloody footprints, she grabbed the lapels of her thin white and lemon dress and ripped it off her body. Immediately she bent down and wiped away all evidence of her shoeprints before crawling back behind the desk. Just as she got out of sight, the door clicked open.

Penelope couldn't see from behind the desk but she could hear. She made out the voices of two people - a male and a female - and the female was Grace.

"Why is this soldier's mouth not taped up?" was her immediate question. 'Shit!' thought Penelope. She hadn't even thought to replace the tape over his mouth. The next voice was the man. It was a bumbling, rambling, panicked voice, much like that of someone in permanent fear.

"I, I don't know Ma'am. I, I, I'm sure I taped it. M, maybe I forgot" he stammered. Penelope could hear him rushing around at that point and she felt his presence just the other side of the desk before hearing the sound of more duct tape being ripped from its roll right above her head. She gasped slightly but it was inaudible. Grace was tutting and sighing and at one point Penelope even thought she heard her smack her face with her palm.

"How's he doing anyway?" she asked a usually endearing question in the most monotone and careless voice.

"All g, good Ma'am. No, no sign of infection. Healing w, well. Should be ready f, f, for the replacement pro, procedure in f, f, four d, d, days." Penelope shivered. Whether it was because she was cold from the fact she was only wearing knickers and shoes, and her body was pressed between the cold metal desk and the even colder tiled walls, or whether it was because of what she was hearing, she wasn't quite sure. It was probably both.

"Good. Now give him some water before you stick that tape back on. We don't want you dying on us now do we? Not when we have a very important task for you to fulfil." Grace directed her speech to the man on the chair who was breathing in heavy short sharp gasps. A quiet slurping sound cut the breathing for a few seconds before it returned at a slightly slower pace. "Let's go, Boyle. I need to check on that waif, Penelope." A few shuffling footsteps followed by the loud clacking of Grace's heels echoed in the room before the door slammed shut. Penelope's heart whacked against the inside of her chest. She had to find her way back to East Wing before Grace got there. But what about her bloody dress? What about the legless man in the chair? She emerged from behind the desk, her breasts exposed, clutching her bloody attire in her shaky hands. She rushed over to the man, with no regard to her nakedness, and removed the fresh tape from his mouth once more.

"Please, don't leave me here. You can't leave me!"

"Shhhhh!" Penelope silenced him. "What's your name?"

"What?"

"What's your name!"

"Sam. Bu-"

"Sam. Look, Sam, I have to leave you here for now, but I promise you I'll come back. I can't even begin to imagine what you've been through but I promise I will not let you go through any more. Please, you have to trust me."

Sam's eyes saddened but Penelope was sure she detected a glimmer of hope deep within them.

"Okay," he sighed, "but please, don't leave me too long." Penelope nodded in agreement and placed her hand on his briefly before exiting the room.

The corridors back were a confusing maze. Penelope was sure she had passed a certain door with a no entry sign on it four times already and she was running as fast as she could. There was no sign of Grace in any of these corridors; Penelope would have had fair warning of her being nearby due to the menacing clunk of her heels. But she did not see her nor even hear her heels in a distant corridor. She must have her own way to and from Sam, Penelope thought. The icy maze of tunnels was beginning to take its toll on her bare bony body but eventually she came across a long hall that seemed familiar to her – it was the link back to the East Wing. At the end of the link was the laundry room which was usually the limit for as far as Penelope needed to go to perform her duties. She began sprinting down the link, her tiny shoes squeaking against the linoleum floor. She halted herself as she reached the laundry room and tried to get her breath back before opening the door. She began fumbling with the handle when she realised – it was locked. Penelope's heart sank. She was standing in the corridor now, mostly naked, with bloody clothes in her hand and she could not get in the laundry room. She punched the door in her frustration and the bang echoed out.

"Shit, shit, shit!" Penelope uttered to herself. She had to think cleverly – and fast. Before she hardly knew it, her aching legs were taking her back to the East Wing wards. She burst through the swing doors of the first ward where heavily sedated men lay in their beds, hardly startled by her presence. She looked around, looked down at her bloody clothes, and then she knew what she had to do. Quickly, she redressed herself then turned and grabbed a pair of scissors from the top draw of the filing cabinet. Furtively, she crept over to the area of the ward where the patients were receiving blood transfusions in preparation for unknown procedures. She raised the scissors up to the height of the first patient's blood transfusion bag. She hesitated for a few moments before she began to make out the distinctive clack of Grace's shoes coming down the corridor.

"I'm sorry," she whispered as she opened the scissors and sliced one blade down the side of the bag. Blood spilled out and Penelope stepped closer to ensure some of this fresh blood was wet on her clothes as it mingled in with Sam's blood. The doors behind her swung open and Penelope instantly switched on her act.

"Oh my! Oh gosh! I'm so sorry!" She cried as she began scrabbling around for bandages and cloths.

"What on earth is going on in here!?" remarked Grace in a much less shocked tone than Penelope would have expected from someone entering such a scene.

"I, I slipped over and knocked this man's drip and blood bag over! Somehow it burst open and the blood has spilled everywhere!" Penelope was impressed with herself and the acting abilities she never knew she had. Grace eyed her suspiciously but Penelope just hung her head and knelt down to start wiping the floor to avoid eye contact.

"You're a clumsy fool sometimes, Penelope." Grace murmured in her sour voice. "Now get this mess cleaned up and I'll come back later when you're done. There should be a spare dress in the laundry room – yours in smothered in blood."

"The laundry room is locked." Penelope spurted without thinking.

"Is it now? And how would you know that seeing as you're not supposed to do the laundry until the end of the day?"

"I erm, I just guessed it's probably locked all day until it gets opened for me to do laundry – right?"

"Right…" affirmed Grace but she didn't seem convinced. "Well I'll go and unlock it early just for today." She turned and sauntered out of the room, her thin black silhouette intimidating Penelope even as it was walking away from her. The doors shut and Penelope dropped her head and sighed with relief. She was still knelt on the floor. Then she felt a warm tickling sensation down the back of her neck. She lifted her head to see the remaining blood dripping out of the bag from the slit in the side. Penelope got up and looked at the man and began to say, "Hold on, I'm going to get a new blood bag for you, hang in there" but as she looked into his eyes, he didn't seem to be there. She felt his wrist for a pulse. He was dead.

14

Arik and Tempestas were almost back to his stilt house. He had never seen it from this angle before. It looked as bleak and small and sad as all the other shabby little huts people now called home. The two had tried to swim mostly beneath the surface on their way back to avoid attracting attention but Arik was getting tired and could barely hold his breath anymore.

"It's okay," he twisted his neck to face Tempestas as they bobbed in the water, "I'll do this last little stretch myself."

"But you can't swim," Tempestas replied with a puzzling look.

"How hard can it be?" grinned Arik. Was he showing off? He felt as though he was trying to impress her but he couldn't be sure. "Besides, you can't risk coming any closer, I've been missing all night and half the day, if anyone sees us both approaching they'll kill you instantly - and I don't want that." Arik added that final bit in a soft voice as he entwined his fingers with hers beneath the water. He didn't look down, but he could feel they were in their bumpy slimy Fem state below the surface. Tempestas tried to hide her shy smile.

"I'll be back for you soon," whispered Arik.

"Don't be long," Tempestas pleaded, and with that Arik disconnected himself from her and began smacking the water with his palms and kicking his legs as hard as he could in an attempt to swim to his deck. His arms were flailing about both over and under the water and it wasn't long before he caught attention.

"Arik!" There was an almighty splash ahead of him. He couldn't make out what was going on with the salty water blurring his vision and blocking his ears but he was sure someone was swimming towards him. He took short sharp gasps of air when he could as he continued splashing. Before he knew it, two big hands clasped his waist and pushed him up so his head was fully out of the water. He wiped his eyes.

"Dad," he spluttered. Morgan pulled a weird twisted face that was a mix of disappointment and relief.

"Hold on to my shoulders," instructed Morgan as he spun round in the water. Arik gripped his dad tight and he could feel him swimming as hard and as fast as he could back to their stilt house.

Arik sat at the table, wrapped in a towel, his hair still dripping. His dad sat opposite him in a fresh dry shirt and a pair of boxers, Vivienne was washing up (although Arik was sure she was only pretending to busy herself), Kai was sitting on the rug playing with his little toy boats and Hugo was round. He was standing up leaning against the worktop behind Morgan, stroking his orange moustache with his thumb and forefinger. The bitter smell of awkwardness infused the salty air. Kai started making engine noises while playing.

"Hush boy!" It was Hugo commanding Kai. Arik hated it when Hugo did that – it wasn't his place. Kai shut up instantly but didn't look up. Instead he continued in silence. Eventually, Morgan spoke.

"Arik, I need you to tell me where you have been. In addition to this I need you to tell me how the heck you're still alive and why you thought it was okay to bugger off in the first place. I'm not angry, I'm relieved you are back - but you sure gave us all a fright. I want you to understand that my boy." While Morgan had assured he wasn't angry, Arik was certain that the tremor in his voice was exactly that – anger. Arik gulped.

"Tempestas. That's her name. I've been with her this whole time. I tried to save Mum's mirror from going in the water –" Morgan glanced at Vivienne at this point but she did not look up, "- but I fell in and she saved me. She took me to this cave where we talked and she told me the reason she spared me is because I was wearing this!" Arik stuck his fist in the air, the shells rattled harmoniously. "It's a bracelet, but it's not just any bracelet, it's full of powers and it stops the Femaestus attacking the wearer or anyone in close vicinity of it!" Arik finally stopped and he was breathing rapidly. His pulse was racing and his forehead was sweating in the panic to get all the information out in the open. Silence settled like a thick layer of dust in the atmosphere. Vivienne had stopped washing up and Kai was staring wide eyed, mouth agape. It was Hugo that made the first response.

"Tssk! I knew this would happen. Being cooped up in here like prisoners! The kid's gone mental."

"Enough, Hugo," Morgan interjected. He took a deep breath followed by a lengthy exhale. "So you're saying you survived… because of a bracelet?"

"Yes, Dad, that's exactly what I am saying." Arik squirmed on his chair, "and we have to take this bracelet to The Mainland and tell them. They may be able to use it somehow to bring safety to our lives. Dad, please, you have to believe me." Arik could feel all the eyes in the room boring into his skin. He felt irritated. He knew his dad would believe him though, if there was so much of a chance it could be true, his dad would believe him. Morgan fumbled with his own fingers for a few moments and stared down at them. Finally, he spoke again.

"Let me see it." Arik removed the bracelet eagerly and handed it over to his dad. Immediately his dad stood up and walked across the room to the tall shelving cabinet. He reached for a box on the top shelf and opened it. Then chucked the bracelet inside and locked it.

"I thought you were more mature than this, Arik," he sighed. Ariks heart sank. Hugo scoffed and Arik saw a grin under his moustache. Rage burned inside him.

"Dad! What are you doing? That bracelet saved my life! Why won't you believe me? If there's so much of a chance that –"

"ENOUGH, Arik," Morgan raised his voice. Arik had never heard him sound so stern. "Go to your room, I don't want to see you again today." His voice cracked slightly. Arik hung his head as his eyes brimmed with tears. As he sauntered out of the room he could hear Hugo mumbling something about magic and craziness and how Morgan had made a good call. Arik sniffed and whispered under his breath, "I'm sorry, Tempestas."

■■ ■ ■ ■

15

Six months passed and everything remained the same as it had been before. Each day Arik and Kai got up, did some studying, helped their mother, played for a while and went to bed. Each day was the same as it had been before except that now Arik thought about Tempestas every single day. The image of her did not fade from his mind. He remembered everything about her; how the depth of her charcoal green eyes absorbed him, how her light bronze hair was so long that it danced about her sapphire waist beneath the water, how her lilac voice melted his muscles and even how hard and bony her slimy hands felt beneath the surface of the water. His heart hurt every time she glided back into his mind. He hadn't mentioned Tempestas or the bracelet again since the day he returned from being with her – his father had made it quite clear it was not to be mentioned again. Every time Hugo came over he treated Arik like *he* was the younger brother. His mother was so far pregnant now and so deep into a depression that he dared not put any more stress on her. It was only Kai who had believed him, but even Kai wouldn't talk about it. In fact, Arik felt like nobody was really talking in the house. He often heard his father consoling his mother at night and what he assumed was her sobbing but that was about it. The family felt disjointed and awkward. The only bonus of this strange atmosphere where nobody was paying any real attention to each other was that Arik had plenty of time to go out on the deck and look for Tempestas. He would regularly just take his binoculars and stroll out the door and nobody would look twice or stop him. Every day he went out, at least once, to try and catch a glimpse of her. He was sure she would be easy to spot as her beauty would radiate across the water and light up the atmosphere. Every day he went out with high hopes and an aching heart. But every day he saw nothing. Nothing but the wide open blue with stilt houses breaking up the emptiness. Nothing ever broke the surface of the water and every day Arik skulked back inside and spent the rest of his day in misery. He went to bed early so he could spend more time dreaming. In his dreams he could be with her.

One evening, while Arik was in his room about to change for bed, he heard his mother make a sound in the kitchen that started off like a groan but developed into a yelp towards the end. He stood still for a few moments then it happened again, this time followed by a clash of pans. "Mum!" he whispered loudly to himself. He threw down the pyjama bottoms he'd been about to put on and dashed out the door. When he got to the kitchen, Morgan was steadying one side of her, trying to lift her off the floor. Kai was already at the sink wetting towels as he didn't go to bed until later than Arik nowadays. Kai turned to face his big brother as he entered the room and Arik could see worry on his little face. He was about to console him when his dad began barking orders,

"Arik! Help me. Roll out that towel on the bed then come and help me get your mother in there." His forehead looked like it was melting and he was puffing air out rapidly. He was struggling. Vivienne was hanging off him like a huge rag doll. Arik got to work. He quickly sprawled the thick grey towel across the bed then sprinted back to the kitchen and nestled beneath his mother's other arm, helping Morgan lift with all his might. Arik's feet squeaked as they slipped against the floor and his mother screamed again – this time it was blood-curdling.

"Come on!" strained Morgan. They dragged her to the bedroom and laid her on the bed – a bit too abruptly but as carefully as they could. She cried out again but this time it seemed to be words.

"Say that again my love," the sickly mixture of sweetness and panic in Morgan's voice only worried Arik further.

"Morgan, the baby, it's, it's going to kill me!" Vivienne threw her head back and screeched. Bluish veins bulged from her neck and forehead. Kai rushed in and placed a cool wet towel on his mummy's head. Tears were flooding his eyes.

"Kai, go, you don't need to be here," Arik instructed his little brother firmly but gently.

"YES I DO!" He yelled back at Arik, initiating the release of the tears that previously sat in his eyes. Arik glanced at his dad.

"Let him stay," Morgan nodded at Arik. There was reluctance and uncertainty in his voice but now was not the time to focus on Kai. Arik turned his attention to his mother's stomach that gave the illusion of increasing in size every time she arched her back in pain. He placed his hands on the bulbous white and veiny balloon in front of him and turned his head to face his mum.

"It's okay mum, you're doing great, everything is going great," he swallowed the lump in his throat.

"Right, Kai, pass that chunk of wood for your mum to bite on. Arik, hold her hand then use your other hand to massage her stomach. I'll be down this end to deliver the baby. Are you ready, boys? Are you ready, Vivienne? You can do this! Ready...and.........PUSH!"

The hour of ear blistering screaming that followed left Arik feeling numb and everyone exhausted. His mum's cries were constant as one flowed into the next until eventually they cut off abruptly. For a few moments it was quiet, aside from Vivienne's heavy breathing and slight whimpering. Arik and Kai stared at their mother whose face looked like it had aged dramatically in the past hour. Her eyes were shut and Arik could tell she was focusing on calming her breathing. She was still alive and Arik sighed inwardly with relief. Then, while Arik and Kai were listening to the blissful sound of their mother's deep breaths, a gentle cry emerged from the end of the bed. Morgan rose to his feet. In his arms was a tiny bluish pink baby, with two arms and two legs. Then Morgan erupted into a flood of tears and said something unexpected, "It's a girl. It's a girl!" Tears surged from his eyes and painted his smile in salty water. Vivienne opened her eyes to see Morgan stepping towards her round the side of the bed.

"What?" she uttered, barely. Kai ran around the bed and Arik leaned over it so they could both see. It was true. In Morgan's arms wriggled a tiny baby girl, with two legs. Right there in front of him was Arik's little sister who was a girl – a real life human girl.

"It can't be," whispered Vivienne, "how can it be?"

"A baby girl hasn't been born with legs, in place of a tail, for over 20 years. I don't know how but you've done it my love. Look at her, she's dainty and beautiful and perfect," Morgan responded to his wife in his loving and calming tone that he was so good at.

"I want to hold her! I want to hold my sister!" Kai piped up suddenly and Morgan laughed. Arik hadn't seen his dad laugh in a long time.

"Woah, son! Hold on, let your mother hold her first – she did all the hard work after all." With that, Morgan rested his daughter onto Vivienne's chest. Just as the baby girl stopped crying, Vivienne started. Tears of joy, and confusion, flooded her face.

"I don't understand," she sobbed.

"Hey, mum," Arik placed his hand on her shoulder, "don't try to understand right now. Just enjoy the moment. But hurry up because Kai and I want to have a go at holding our baby sister!" He winked at Kai who beamed a grin back at him. Vivienne chuckled which wobbled the baby slightly and her tiny lips curved up into a sort of half-smile.

"Oh my! Oh my, my little girl. My little girl. My happy little girl." Vivienne was crying almost uncontrollably but she was radiating energy and happiness. Morgan had not stopped smiling and, in that moment, Arik couldn't remember a time when he had ever felt happier and full of so much love. Then Morgan ruffled Kai's hair and put his hand out across the bed to shake Arik's. "Well done boys. You helped your mum bring your beautiful little sister into this world. We couldn't have done it without you. I'm proud of you both." Morgan nodded at Arik as he shook his hand. Arik felt as though he was about to burst with pride, excitement and happiness. He was on top of the world and nothing could ever bring him down again.

16

Penelope splashed cold water onto her face. She lifted her head and peered at her bone-grey reflection in her tiny bathroom mirror. She rubbed her eyes and smoothed back her hair as she inhaled for a sigh. 'Come on,' she told herself, 'you can do this.' It was the morning after her day of discovery at S.T.A.B. and she was urging herself into work. Not because it was her job and she had to go in anyway – but because a man's life was at stake. Sam's life. And now that she had accidentally taken the life of another innocent man she felt the aching need to do something good more than ever. She turned the cold tap back on and let the water run over her wrists for a few moments more. She wondered how many other people's lives might be in danger – or already ended. She always knew there was something suspicious about S.T.A.B. but she had never really known what. Grace was more of a monster than Penelope could ever have imagined. The image of the thick fish tails pulsating in their tubes returned to her. They were armoured like tanks and, Penelope assumed, were going to be used as soldiers' modes of transport and weaponry just as tanks were. Was she overthinking things? No, she knew what she saw. Sam's tearful dilated eyes stared at her in her mind. She quickly shut the tap off and as she did so a huge explosion boomed through the air outside. Penelope darted to the window and looked outside from her 25th floor flat. She noticed nothing at first but then, as she surveyed the skyline, she saw dark grey smoke billowing out from the S.T.A.B. building just at the end of her road. 'Shit,' she murmured to herself and grabbed her keys and coat and ran to the elevator.

As Penelope walked up the road towards the S.T.A.B. building she observed a chaotic scene of fire engines and police. Crowds gathered for the excitement and

Penelope could barely shoulder her way through. All the while Penelope had assumed it was probably a gas explosion or some kind of faulty electrics had created it – but then she saw the men in bio suits. Seven or eight of them were marching in carrying some kind of equipment Penelope hadn't seen before.

"Excuse me," she tapped a police officer on the shoulder, "excuse me, I work here. Can I get through please?"

"Sorry ma'am, the building is off limits. I have been told not to let anyone in for the rest of the day."

"But I have to-"

"Ma'am, you're not going in."

"Please, you don't understand, there's a man in there and-"

"There were loads of men in there love, ain't going to change a thing about you getting in." Penelope huffed but calmed herself. She peered up at the building. There was no physical damage to the front of the building or the East Wing. She knew the East Wing had a damaged window round the back and so she decided to sneak round that way. As she scuttled round the side, weaving her way through the crowd, she thought about the rude police officer and how she was grateful he had interrupted her. For all she knew, he was in Grace's pocket. If they really were creating an army of mutants at S.T.A.B. to fight off the Fems then anyone in a position of power probably knew about it – and knew Grace. The last thing Penelope needed was Grace finding out she was on to her.

Penelope reached the back of the East Wing and to her relief it wasn't being guarded. She knew it wouldn't be given there was no entrance there. She hauled one of the industrial bins across the tarmac and positioned it beneath the broken window. The smashed area wasn't big enough for her to fit through so she removed her coat and wrapped it round her hand before thrashing the remaining glass away. Before long, she was inside.

The corridors felt emptier than usual. The dark orange walls felt as though they had gone from warm to burnt. The black silhouettes that swirled up the walls were no longer elegant and inviting but instead loomed like rotting vines, threatening to choke anyone who dared walk the corridor. Penelope quickened her pace – partly due to the eeriness of the place but also because she had to find Sam. Before long she reached the laundry room. She briefly checked in on her ward as though some part of her cared for the men that were in there. They were fine and nothing had changed. She continued on past the laundry room and down the corridor that had led her to Sam previously. As she navigated her way through the twists and turns the smell of burning grew increasingly stronger. She turned a corner to find a passageway filled lightly with smoke. Was this the route she took before? She couldn't be sure. The smoke was getting heavier and it was hard to see through the fogginess. She decided to feel her way. She placed one hand on the cool tiles of the wall and used the other to hold her scarf over her mouth and nose in an attempt to help her breathe but the smoke was still infiltrating her lungs. She spluttered a few times before building up the air required to call out for Sam. There was no response. She called again but erupted into a coughing fit. She stood for a while until it passed then continued. Suddenly the feeling against her palm and fingers was no longer wall but a door. Penelope felt for the handle but it opened easier than she anticipated and she fell through it into the room. Awkwardly she scrambled to her feet and hurriedly shut the door behind her as she realised it had been keeping the smoke out of the room. She paused for a few seconds to regain her breath. As she turned round she was met with two emotions; delight, from realising she had stumbled across the right room, and relief to see that Sam was still in it, slumped lifelessly in the chair. Her dramatic entrance hadn't startled him though and his eyes were closed. "Please, God," Penelope mumbled to herself as she dashed over to him. She pressed her fingers against his skeletal wrist and lowered her face so that it was almost touching his lilac lips. A breath. A pulse. Although both faint, it was enough for Penelope to know that Sam was still alive and she could get him out of there.

"Sam, it's me, it's Penelope. I'm here. Sam!" Penelope shook his shoulders gently with desperation. "Sam, I came back for you but I'm going to need you to help me get you out of here. Please, Sam." Penelope's voice broke as she started to weep. A few stray tears seeped from her eyes and speckled Sam's face. Penelope sniffed. "Sam," she whispered once more.

"Yes?" A voice that Penelope could only describe as weak and dying responded to her. She wiped her face to see Sam's mouldy yellow eyes peering up at her. She smiled.

"Come on, there's no time to waste. I need you to use all your strength to roll over onto this bed," Penelope scuttled over to a hospital bed pushed up in the corner of the room and briskly wheeled it over to him. Then she darted round the other side of the bed and locked her hands beneath Sam's back and ribs in a bid to help him roll. She pushed with every fibre in her little body. She felt Sam pulling with every deteriorating fibre of his. Together they managed to get him on the hospital bed and Penelope pounced for the door. She flung it open with one hand whilst she pulled the bed through with the other. As soon as they entered the corridor Sam began wheezing and spluttering in the smoke so Penelope covered his entire body and face with the white bedding. That's when Penelope knew how she was going to get him past everyone outside.

"Sam, soon we will be out of this smoke, and once we are *do not* make a sound or move again until I say so," she instructed through the sheets. He didn't reply but Penelope just had to pray that he had understood her.

Penelope wheeled the bed back through the winding corridors and past the broken window where she had made her entrance. She was looking for a fire escape that she'd easily be able to open from the inside. While S.T.A.B. appeared to break many rules, it seemed to be hot on having a sufficient amount of fire exits and it wasn't long before she found one. She stationed Sam to the side as she levered the heavy grey bar on the door. No alarm sounded.

The door clicked open and fresh air and sunlight rolled inside. Penelope inhaled the relief and smiled as she began wheeling Sam out away from S.T.A.B. Pushing the bed back past the crowd of people was no issue. Nobody even turned to look at her as they were too concerned with what was happening in the building. The commotion provided her with cover for the first part; and for the rest of the walk to her apartment building, the few people who did glance at her probably just assumed she was working and helping remove the deceased.

Before long, Penelope had Sam positioned in her front room. The bed seemed much bigger in her small apartment and there was barely room for her to squeeze down the side of it. She pulled the covers back from Sam's face and Penelope could see that he was only just hanging on to his life. She acted fast, digging out all her medical supplies that she had accumulated when training at the hospital. First she sedated him so that he was pain free and his heart did not have to work so hard. He was safe now. His life was in her hands only – and she was not letting him go. She removed the sticky sheets that clung to what remained of his legs. Two yellowing and bruised stumps, covered in pus and blood, festering and decaying before her very eyes. Penelope gagged. The smell was putrid and it clogged her nostrils. She did not throw up this time though. Instead, she took an even deeper breath in and began cleaning and cutting away at Sam's tainted flesh.

17

Terra was three days old. Vivienne and Morgan had taken the first couple of days to decide her name. Arik supposed they hadn't really thought about girl's names for the entire nine months. Terra was beautiful. She brought so much love and light to their previously morbid little hut. Arik stretched in his bed as he heard his mother giggling and cooing over Terra downstairs. Life was good. Then he heard something else.

"Morg! How you doing old boy?" Great. The false and pretentious voice of Hugo bellowed from the floor below. "Come on, has your lovely wife had this baby yet?" He's just an irritation, Arik told himself, just a tiny inconspicuous scratch on the surface of his new found happiness. He wasn't going to let Hugo bother him today Arik thought as he went downstairs - he may even make the effort to smile at Hugo, be the bigger man.

But as soon as Arik entered the kitchen Hugo shut him down.

"Wahey, here he is, little fantasy boy. Hey, how's it going in magic bracelet land kid?" Hugo released a snort from beneath his orange moustache like the big fat pig that he was. Arik looked down at his feet. He didn't want to be as childish as he saw Hugo. He lifted his head again and looked at his Dad for support but Morgan was just gazing at Terra who was swaddled up and being held by Hugo. He didn't like him holding his little sister.

"Can I just get a quick cuddle with my sister, please? I haven't said good morning to her yet." Arik asked politely as he leaned in to take Terra. Then Hugo pulled away. He turned so his shoulder was in Arik's way, blocking Terra completely.

"Hey, hey kid. I've only just gotten a cuddle myself. Calm down." Arik felt his cheeks redden.

"I just want to cuddle my sister." He growled through gritted teeth. Suddenly he felt himself lunge for his sister but Hugo stretched out his big tartan covered arm and wiped Arik out as his face crashed into Hugo's elbow.

"What the hell is going on!?" cried Vivienne who sounded as if she had only just entered the room but had in fact witnessed the whole thing. Arik looked again at his Dad for support. His nose was throbbing.

"Arik you get to see your sister all day every day. Hugo has journeyed over here to meet her for the first time. Why are you being so selfish?" Morgan's words stabbed Arik over his entire body. A sense of betrayal lifted the hairs on his arms and the back of his neck. Arik was seething. He got up and wiped his face before storming off and slamming the kitchen door. He went to the shelves and climbed to the top, reached for the box, smashed it open and grabbed the bracelet. Then Kai walked in.

"Where are you going, Arik?"

"Out. Don't worry about me. Just be a big boy and look after your little sister ok?" Arik marched out of the front door, across the deck and dived into the water.

The cool water chilled Arik's burning face. It swirled round his body and between his fingers. It soothed him. He hadn't thought through what he was going to do when he could no longer hold his breath but in that moment the water was holding him and he felt peace. The small shells clinking together on his wrist sounded loud and chunky beneath the surface. They jangled in time with the rhythm of his heart which was slowing as it craved oxygen. He could hear his heartbeat deep inside where the blood thumped in his ears. He needed to breathe. He began to push the water back with his arms as he'd seen Tempestas do. He wasn't sure what to do with his legs but kicking seemed like a good idea. Soon he was travelling back towards the surface. He was swimming! He broke through to the open air and gasped. He continued to kick his legs and push the water down and was able to keep his head above water. Suddenly one of his feet kicked something too hard to be water. Panic consumed him. He began to kick harder. Whether in an attempt to stay afloat or to kick whatever it was in the water with him he wasn't sure. Then a familiar feeling caused his spine to shudder - a hand on his back. He craned his next round and out of the water came the striking beauty of Tempestas. Arik's heart inflated. His blood fizzed inside him and his eyes widened as his throat tightened. He seemed to have lost the ability to speak.

"Hey you," she smiled.

"Hi," Arik croaked.

"What are you doing out here? Did you take the bracelet to someone? Did you come back to find me?"

Tempestas' questions flew at Arik and bounced right off him. He was entranced by her. He wanted, so badly, to respond to her and seem unaffected by her but it was no use. Her beauty took his breath away. Eventually, he found the courage to say the only thing he wanted to say to her in that moment.

"You are so beautiful." He uttered. "I've thought about you every day. I've even been going out onto the deck in the hope to see you. Where have you been?" Arik was certain he saw Tempestas blush.

"I have been floating around waiting for you," she smiled - then her lips turned down at the corners, "did you not take the bracelet?"

"It's complicated," Arik sighed, "nobody believed me." He hung his head in shame. Then he felt Tempestas cup his face and lift it as she had done before in the cave.

"Hey, don't worry. Come. I know something that'll cheer you up," she winked.

Tempestas swam to a cave at the edge of The Mainland, Arik clinging on to her shoulders all the way.

"The humans don't come around here," Tempestas assured. Arik hauled himself up onto a smooth, flat rock so that his feet were still just dipped in the silky water. He looked around at the jade stone, grey rocks, brown sand and plain shells. This was simply a cave. Why did Tempestas think it would cheer him up?

"So… nice cave," he muttered, trying to stifle his sarcasm.

"Don't be silly, this isn't what I wanted to show you," Tempestas giggled. Then she locked eyes with Arik with a stern face. "I need you to kiss me."

"What?" Arik spluttered, almost falling off his rock.

"There's this technique some of the weaker Femaestus use to pull men down into the water if they're not very good at fighting. They use their beauty to persuade the men to kiss them so that they too can breathe underwater and they remain to see the girls in their full beautiful form while under the surface - and it works! However it's only for a limited period of time. Once the men have been swimming around deep under the water with this beautiful temptress, falling in to an intense state of enchantment, being lulled into a false sense of security, the ability wears off and they drown before they can reach the surface again."

Arik gulped.

"And how do I know that's not what you're going to do with me?" He chuckled, but worry laced his voice.

"Do you not trust me by now?" asked Tempestas, with sadness in her eyes. "Plus you have this." She stroked the bracelet on his wrist then glided her finger down onto his palm, tracing the lines on his hand. Electricity zapped through Arik's body. He leaned in, thrust his other hand up into her wet hair to hold the back of her head… and kissed her. As his lips drifted over hers with varying pressure, Tempestas gently pulled Arik down into the water. Their kiss continued. As they sank slowly deeper, Arik held her tighter. He couldn't kiss her enough. He didn't want it to end. But he needed air. He opened his eyes and pulled carefully away from Tempestas' salty lips. She nodded at him and smiled. So he inhaled. It worked. Tempestas looked even more breath-taking below the water now. Her golden hair swirled and danced daintily about her face and body. Her smile melted Arik's heart and her eyes lit up the ocean. She circled round and took his hand as if to guide him somewhere. Arik obediently followed.

After swimming for about five minutes but still in relatively shallow water, Arik began to spy something to his right, just at the base of the cliffside of The Mainland.

They were far away from the cave now already and Arik sensed there were probably guards patrolling the land above them. Still, Arik figured he was quite unnoticeable under the water and began to swim over to whatever the bulky grey smudge was lying at the bottom of the cliff. As he approached, his vision began to blur slightly as the water seemed to become less pure. It was tainted with fine particles of which Arik couldn't determine the source. The water appeared to blacken as the particles thickened and soon Arik felt as though he was swimming through a toxic sludge. He was still breathing but he could feel the water entering and leaving his lungs as a thick treacle now whereas it'd felt just like air previously. Arik wafted and batted the water with his palms to try and make a clearing. Suddenly, a circular patch cleared and staring back at Arik through the clearing was a greying skull. A slight yelp escaped him as he wafted away more sludge. More and more skulls grinned and glared back at him. As he rose in the water he saw it was not just one row but layers and layers of bodies in a heap that became more clothed with flesh as he ascended the pile. Suddenly there was a tug on his leg. Arik was flung down and backwards rapidly as he wailed in fear. He couldn't get the angle to twist his body. What was yanking him? He was flying through the water now, out of the sludge, through the dusty water and eventually back in the open crystal blue. The swimming stopped, and he was released. He turned around to see Tempestas giving him a look of disappointment. Arik lowered his eyes in apology but Tempestas took him by the chin and smiled. She waved her hand in the opposite direction, beckoning him, this time he followed obediently and wasn't going to swim astray.

As they swam on a blurry figure of something brown and bulky began to materialise in front of them. As they drifted closer, Arik realised it was an old shipwreck embedded firmly in the sand. It was huge and magnificent and loomed over the two of them, filling Arik with awe. He looked down. The sun beamed through the crystal water, illuminating the multitude of precious gifts around him. Tiny aquatic flowers with raindrop petals glittered in the sunlight. Lime green plants and butter yellow fish danced and played and twirled around him, occasionally kicking up grains of pure white sand that twinkled in the penetrative sunrays. A loud clanking noise snapped him out of his blissful trance. Every miniscule sound was intensified in the water and the metallic vibrations chimed into Arik's skull. The sound was coming from a chunky rusty chain, laden with an inch of thick slimy algae, dangling from one side of the ship. Arik tracked it to the end where it was swirled up like a giant snake in the sand. Minute blue fish zipped in and out of the loops with ease and speed, guiding their perfectly streamline bodies through the bulky obstacle. Strewn across the seabed were dozens of dainty opalescent shells shimmering in glittering golds and sparkling silvers. The beauty that surrounded him consumed Arik and he almost forgot about Tempestas amidst all his wonder. He flapped his way into an upright position to look for her but as he scouted the area she was nowhere in sight. He panicked briefly until he caught a flash of her luminous blue tail whipping about inside the ship. As quickly as his inelegant swimming would allow, he hurried after her. As he neared the entrance to the wreck (which was simply a cavernous hole near the bottom which Arik presumed must have sunken her) it became more shadowy and a little foreboding. The pressure of the water caused the remaining wood around him to moan painfully as the gentle current pulled and pushed its aching planks. Once inside, Arik allowed his eyes to adjust to the gloominess for a few minutes. As his sight became clearer he was able to make out some of the interior items; a huge rotting table that looked like it once seated 12 men was laying on its side, a few cloudy liquor bottles were deep-rooted in the greyish sand that lined the floor and in the middle of the space sat an old ornate chest with solid iron bolts on the corners and deeply carved intricate patterns adorning the wood. But it was what was atop the chest that really made Ariks heart thud with admiration – the beauty of Tempestas. There she was, just sitting on the chest, her magnificent tail relaxed down the side and looped round the base. Arik's eyes traced upwards, past her tiny waist and her exposed small pinkish breasts, beyond her protruding collarbones and glistening eyes, right up to where her golden hair flared from her head and twirled about her face effortlessly, coiling up at the ends. She truly was a picture of beauty and before Arik knew it he had swum up to her to within an inch of her face. He placed one hand tenderly round her waist, cupping the small of her back, and the other on her scaly lap. Her scales felt as hard and as heavy as granite but he imagined the weight of them was unnoticeable in the water. He lifted his head slightly so that his lips were just touching Tempestas' piquant pout. Then he launched with full emotion and passion. He kissed Tempestas so firmly yet so gently. He kissed her so deeply yet so lightly. He wanted to project his feelings for her yet didn't want to suffocate her. That's when Arik realised he needed to stop for air – but it wasn't the kissing that was leaving him unable to breathe. As he pulled away to inhale his lungs took on a heavy influx of water. He spluttered then naturally tried to breathe again. He felt his body begin to convulse and looked at Tempestas whose skin was beginning to melt. Her teeth were becoming jagged and dark grey bone was becoming exposed from beneath her skin. Her ice blue eyes were turning black as night but Arik could still make out the expression on her face – it was panic. Then he felt her snatch his hand and he was yanked in a sideways direction. Although his sight was darkening he could make out leaving the ship and flitting past the chain, he could make out zooming back past all the multi-coloured fish. Then they began to ascend with lightning speed. He could feel the strength in Tempestas' tail pushing them closer to air. Within seconds they broke the surface and Tempestas hauled Arik up on to the rock he'd been on previously. He coughed and spluttered, water spewing from both his mouth and nose. He took a while to regain his breath.

"Thought you were going to eat me for a second back there," he half joked. Tempestas' face dropped and Arik saw a bit of sadness, but mostly disappointment, in her eyes.

"Arik, do you still not trust me?" Arik could have kicked himself for saying something so stupid.

"I'm sorry," he whispered, "that was incredible." Tempestas' eyes lit up again and her smile tugged at Arik's heart. Then Arik remembered the stack of bodies he'd discovered.

"Tempestas, what were all those bodies in the water?" Arik felt almost ashamed to ask. He felt like he knew the answer - after all they were human bodies so it had to have something to do with the Femaestus... right? Tempestas sighed and hung her head.

"You just don't know anything do you, silly human," she half joked – but only half, "that's a graveyard."

"Yes," Arik piped up, a little too defensively, "because the bodies have to go somewhere after you girls kill them." Tempestas daggered a look of scorn at Arik that he felt prick his skin all over. He cowered from her glare.

"That is a *human* graveyard created by *humans*. There's no room left on The Mainland to live Arik and certainly no room left to DIE. There's tons of them, scattered all around the edge. You die on The Mainland, you get dumped in the sea. You die on the stilts, you get dumped in the sea. There's more death in these waters than just *us* Arik." Tempestas spat each syllable like a sour snake. Arik felt so small. He curled into his knees, ashamed. "I'm sorry," he whispered. There was silence for a few minutes until Tempestas spoke.

"At least we got back in time to watch the sunset," she lightly chuckled, clearly trying to lift the mood.

"Yes at least – wait, what?" Arik cut himself short. Sunset! How long had he been gone? "Oh no. It's so late. Tempestas I should go back," he cried, trying not to sound desperately concerned.

"It's ok, I understand, I'll take you back," she smiled.

By the time Arik had regained his strength and hitchhiked the journey back clinging to Tempestas' shoulders, the sweet sun had dipped below the horizon. It was dark but beautiful and peaceful and quiet. There was no sound except the gentle hush of the low waves. He turned to Tempestas in the water and kissed her once more.

"I'll see you again soon," he promised. Tempestas nodded in the silence. "I didn't want today to end." As Arik gazed into her eyes, attempting to fill her with hope, he became aware of a distant rumbling sound. Tempestas heard it too. They both turned their heads to look around as it rapidly became increasingly louder.

"That's a speed boat," Arik confirmed, "why would there be speed boat coming out here? Especially at this time of night?"

"Perhaps they're looking for you?" Tempestas suggested.

"No. No, my family have no way of contacting The Mainland, only when my dad gets on the morning row boat to work. It must be for something else."

When the thunderous buzzing was almost on top of them, they spied not just one but four white speed boats grinding to a halt… right outside Arik's hut. Aboard the boats were soldiers - with guns.

"They must be for you Arik –"

"No! Something's wrong. Tempestas get me as close as you can then go! Do you hear me? Make yourself scarce as soon as you can."

Tempestas flipped to it. She soared right up behind the boat that was at the back and Arik clambered up as the soldiers alighted onto his deck. He glanced back at the water but Tempestas had already disappeared into the blackness. He turned back to see his front door being booted down by one of the men. The door crumbled and the soldiers piled in. His mother screamed. Terra began to cry. Morgan was bellowing and Kai was screeching.

"Let go of me!" Arik heard his mother try to shout although it was muffled. Arik ran for the door but as he did two soldiers crashed back through it, his mother in their grip.

"Mum!" Arik cried.

"Arik!" she burst into tears. Arik imagined it was partly with relief at seeing him. Morgan suddenly crashed through the doorway behind them, brandishing an old baseball bat.

"Dad! Dad, what's going on?" Arik sobbed.

"LET GO OF MY WIFE!" Morgan yelled as he clocked one of the soldiers round the face. Blood spattered up the side of the house.

"Restrain him!" commanded one of the other soldiers. Four or five men proceeded to pounce on Morgan. Arik suddenly realised Terra's crying wasn't coming from inside anymore but outside. He swung round to see one of the soldiers darting across the deck with a bundle of blankets with Terra swaddled inside.

"Hey! Where do you think you're going with my sister!?" Arik roared. He ran across the deck and leapt on the man's back and began punching him repeatedly in the side of the head. The man stumbled and began to drop the blankets. Eventually Terra fell from his grip but she did not hit the floor.

"Kai!" Arik shot a quick smile at his brother. He'd caught her! "Take her inside!" He instructed.
Arik eyed Kai all the way to the door where he was suddenly confronted by two more soldiers. One slapped Kai round the face while the other plucked Terra from his skinny little arms. Morgan was still wrestling on the floor. Vivienne was screaming from the boat that she was now on. Arik punched and flexed and screamed and cried until his throat was raw and his eyes bled tears. Then he felt a blow round the side of his head. His ears rang and the force of the clout caused him to fall to the deck. Once his ears stopped ringing, the familiar rumbling sound of the speedboat engines returned to him. He pressed his hands to the floor to lift himself but blood was gushing from his nose and he flopped back onto the deck. Then one of the soldiers yelled.   "Femaestus! Let's go, let's go, let's go!"

Arik twisted round to see the men, who were previously restraining his dad, now fleeing from him in the direction of the boats. He could see his mum being held on one boat and the soldier who had Terra was on another. As the last few men ran in single file to jump aboard the final boat, a shattering, crashing sound, like a bomb made of ice, exploded into the chilled night air, followed by a howling scream that made Arik's blood freeze within his veins. Fear rooted every man to the spot as their eyes rolled around frantically in the dark. Nobody could tell which direction it had come from. Nobody could see much past the edge of the deck and the lights on the boats. Then, without any further warning, the silhouette of a slender body shadowed by a solid tail soared from the water and into the night sky, briefly blocking the moon like an eclipse. Water sprayed down, soaking everyone. The figure flipped round when it reached its highest point and began spiralling back towards one of the boats. The speed was remarkable. Nobody had time to move. As it slid back into the water at the other edge of the boat, both sides of her full-bodied tail snapped round the throats of two of the soldiers and whipped them overboard, dragging them down into the darkness.

"GO! GO!" yelped one of the men who didn't seem so intimidating anymore. But before Arik could get to his feet the boats sped off into the black night.

"Mum!" Arik's cry echoed out into the emptiness. He began to sob. Morgan peeled Kai's limp body off the deck and carried him inside. Arik followed them in. "Is he okay?"

"He's fine; he's just been knocked out." Morgan's voice was blunt. Arik couldn't make out whether he was upset, angry, confused or all three combined.

"Dad, you know this was Hugo don't you?" Arik questioned quietly. Morgan sat silent. Arik's anger began to rise inside him. "Dad? Come on, you know this was Hugo. You can't possibly think they found out any other way!"

"I don't know what I think at the moment, Arik!" He snapped back.

"Yes you do! You just don't want to admit it. I bet he's made some deal with the people on The Mainland. I know it was him dad and so do you! Stop trying to see the good in people all the time-"

Morgan slapped Arik hard across the cheek. Arik was stunned into silence. The two sat there for the next few minutes without uttering a single word until Kai woke up.

"Hey, son," Morgan soothed, "how are you feeling?"

"My head hurts a little," croaked Kai. He then peered at the two of them; Arik with his crimson cheek and Morgan with his puffed out chest, and begged, "Please don't you two fight." At this Morgan dropped his head down into his hands. Arik could tell from the lines creasing at the sides of dirty cheeks that he was screwing his face up behind his palm-shield in an attempt not to cry. He took a few deep breaths before lifting his head again, revealing his reddened face and eyes. He then clutched his two boys, one in each arm, and held them in tight.

"I love you boys; you know that right?" Arik was surprised by Morgan's choice of words.

"Dad, we know. Now we need to go get mum and Terra back." Why did Arik feel he had to be the grown up all the time?

"Boys, listen to me. Out there...it's a dangerous world. I am going to get your mum back as soon as day breaks – alone."

"No!" Kai yelled immediately. "We are coming with you!"

"He's right," Arik could hardly believe he was siding with Kai over his dad, "we're coming with you. And we can't go in the daylight dad; the soldiers would spot us coming a mile off and take us out."

"So you suggest we go at night do you, Arik, the time when the Femaestus are harder to see and fend off?"

"Yes, that's exactly what I suggest." Arik replied sternly. Morgan half laughed.

"Stop laughing at him dad! He's right! He's been out there!" Kai was speaking up too.

"It's true dad, that Femaestus that took down that soldier? I *know* her. We're...friends. She was protecting us!" Arik was almost shouting at his dad. Morgan kept on shaking his head and sighing. He lolled his head forward again, this time with his thumb and fingers supporting his leathery forehead. He was staring at the floor, thinking. Arik and Kai both knew to keep quiet for a while and allow him to process his thoughts as well as gather his emotions.

Eventually he raised his head slightly and looked at the boys through his brow bone. He cleared his throat, ready for his firm soldier-like voice to follow.

"Okay boys, you can come with me to get your mum and sister back. Admittedly I will probably need your help. But I am not risking losing either of you. We go at night, I agree, but if we see one of those things I want you to know that I am slaying it there and then without any hesitation. Are we clear?" Both Arik and Kai gulped but nodded at their father in agreement. Besides, Arik knew that none would come near for an attack so long as he had his bracelet.

18

There was nothing on the TV. Penelope flicked through the few channels she had but every one was the same; each channel displayed a similar news studio set up only with slightly different colour schemes and each one had a different newsreader interviewing the same old man who had tangerine skin, drastically contrasting white hair and a dapper charcoal suit. The only topic ever discussed was the future of The Mainland. Penelope scoffed at the word 'future'. A whole 48 hours had passed since she got Sam back to her apartment and treated him but, while he had already started to heal nicely, he still hadn't woken up. She wondered what could have come of Sam's 'future' had she not rescued him. She pushed herself out of her modern grey tub chair and sighed. As she sauntered over to Sam she grabbed the last slice of 'Chocolate Fake' off the counter. It was called chocolate 'fake' rather than cake as there was no room left for livestock on land anymore so there were no eggs, no milk - not even any flour as there were no fields left. Penelope wasn't actually sure what her Chocolate Fake was made of but it sure tasted and smelled of good rich chocolate and so she had decided long ago she'd rather not question the source of its ingredients. She waltzed back through her glamorous apartment; when people realised they could no longer build 'out' they had decided to build 'up' so her apartment on the 25th floor was one of the newest. Mostly everything was clean clinical white with the odd light grey addition here and there such as a chair or the counter. Penelope had fake plants dotted around everywhere to remind her of what used to be - back when there was space for grass and trees and fields. She squeezed in between Sam and the wall and sat on the edge of the bed. She was tediously cutting chunky bites off her cake and ladling them into her mouth when something brushed against her thigh. There it was again. She glanced down to see Sam's hand laying palm up like a dead beetle and as lifeless as one too. Had she imagined it? Had it always been that way up? Penelope couldn't recall in what position she had left his large hands. Even while they were motionless they still looked strong. She gazed at the robust limp hand without blinking as though she thought it might spring to life if she stared hard enough. Nothing. Penelope let out a long deep breath and reverted her gaze back to what remained of her cake. Suddenly a distressing coughing sound disturbed the atmosphere in her apartment. She jumped, throwing her plate of cake at the wall where it shattered to pieces. She turned round. Sam was looking at her wide eyed. He stopped coughing and instead breathed in deeply before saying, "Well that was a waste of a nice bit of Chocolate Fake."

After the two had shared a giggle, and Penelope had calmed herself down from Sam's dramatic awakening, they both fell into a sort of silence. It wasn't an awkward silence but the realisation had just hit Penelope that the two had never really even spoken properly before. She had been waiting two days for this beautiful man to wake up to ask him so many questions and suddenly found herself lost for words. She couldn't possibly jump straight into question time! The poor man had only just woken up and his last full memory was probably having both his legs savagely removed. All these thoughts were whizzing through her mind and her anxiety to speak was becoming overwhelming when finally, Sam spoke instead.

"I guess I owe you a thank you. I don't know how I will ever thank you enough but I want you to know I am grateful." His voice was viscous and flowed smoothly down her ear canals. It was blissful to hear him speak however she still could not find the ability to do so herself. Sam became aware of this and so continued in a bid to ease her. "You know, I think it was the smell of the chocolate cake that woke me up," he smiled, "as it's one of my favourites out of the 'foods' we have left to choose from nowadays." Again, they both laughed. Penelope's muscles relaxed and her heart beat heavy but slower.

Tentatively, she placed a small hand on Sam's wide bristly jaw.

"I'm so glad you're ok," she whispered and almost began to weep. She felt her eyes welling and her throat swelling – but she did not cry. In fact, she was excited to spend a couple of days at home with a now fully conscious Sam. S.T.A.B. was still closed and Penelope had received an email explaining that it would be for another day or two. There was no mention in the email as to what had happened. Penelope sidled down to the bottom of the bed and kicked off the breaks. She wheeled Sam gently into her front room and positioned him in front of the television.

"There isn't much to watch," she said.

"It's okay," Sam soothed, "it's not like there's much else I can do right now." He laughed but his attempt at a joke did not quell the ache in his voice. Penelope's heart wilted. The sympathy she felt for Sam devastated her to the very core. She gazed at him as he watched the television and began to question whether she had even done the right thing by saving him. As she surveyed the expressions on his face she noticed his eyes begin to widen and his whole face drop. He began to breathe rapidly. Penelope threw her stare to the television where she saw the same old studio and the same old guy as always but now there was someone sitting next to him. It was Grace. As desperately as Penelope wanted to hear what she had to say, she could see that just the sight of her was filling Sam with trepidation.

"I'll turn it off," she said as she fumbled for the remote.

"No, it's fine, really. I need to see this." Sam looked at Penelope and nodded with reassurance. As he did so her hand landed on the remote and so she turned up the volume. Grace's voice began to poison the air.

"Well as you know, at S.T.A.B. we have been trying valiantly to find ways of curing deadly diseases and terminal illnesses but also we have been researching ways of combatting our current lifestyle crisis we find ourselves in. Our experiments and procedures have been put on hold for a few days due to a gas explosion in part of the building. People have raised concerns as they saw the men in biosuits entering the S.T.A.B. a couple of days ago but I can reassure you all that these were purely deployed just in case there was any contamination and diseases needed to be contained. The building and everyone in it is now safe."

Penelope felt sick.

"The only worry we have now is that one of our many patients has not been accounted for."

Penelope choked.

"We are very concerned about the welfare of this man. He has recently undergone a double leg amputation and could be in a dazed and confused state. We believe he has had help leaving the building so please, if you are the person 'helping' this man, let me inform you that you are doing quite the opposite. This man needs special care and treatment that we can only provide here at S.T.A.B. We will be sending soldiers out looking for you."

Penelope launched from her seat, snatched a vase off the table and hurled it at the wall.

"That *bitch!"* She roared. "I'm going to kill her, I swear!" Penelope's hands were in her hair scraping at her scalp. Her blood was sizzling beneath her skin and her legs were trembling with anger. She had never felt so violently furious in her life.

"Hey, Penelope, it's okay-"

"It's not okay. Nothing is okay. She can't get away with this! She can't, she can't treat people like this and lie to the public that way. She can't send *soldiers* out for people like hunting dogs. She..." Penelope trailed off as fear consumed her and tears began to gush from her eyes. She slapped her hands over her face and cried.

"Come here," Sam instructed softly. Penelope dragged her hands down from covering her face and ambled over to the bed. She climbed in next to Sam, curled her body round his and nestled into his torso as he put his great arms around her.

"Just look at what she's done to you," Penelope spoke quietly now, her voice muffled by her face being pressed into Sam's chest. The rise and fall of it began to soothe her. "She knows it was me, doesn't she?"

"If she knew it was you, Penelope, soldiers would have busted in here two days ago. She has no idea yet but I know she will send them here just to check soon. I will need to get out of here."

"And go where? There's nowhere else to go, Sam. There's nowhere to run to, nowhere to hide." Penelope peered up at him with worried eyes. Sam sighed.

"Then I guess I'll just have to hand myself back over."

"What?"

"It's the only way I'm going to be able to keep you safe. It terrifies me to think what Grace would do to you if she found out you helped me escape." Sam's words filled Penelope with fury.

"If you honestly think that I'm going to just let you go back there, after all this, then you need to get to know me better. It's Grace that's going down – not you. We just need to think of a plan. Together." Penelope felt like the past few years had caused some kind of manic animal to grow inside her and it was finally ready to be unleashed. She was no longer timid - no longer scared. She was ready to start taking down her prey.

19

Morgan had spent the entire day, following the kidnap of his wife and daughter, pulling up the planks of the deck from round the house and fashioning some kind of raft. Although it was small, it looked sturdy and Arik knew they would be safe on it. Morgan didn't seem so sure. As dusk began to fall, Morgan turned to Arik with a doubtful look in his eye.

"This isn't safe enough," he mumbled, "us three, on this thing, at night. The Fems will just hook us in the water as easy as plucking candy from a baby." He was shaking his head profusely. "I've changed my mind. I'll have to go alone."

"Dad, the sun is almost set. You can't change your mind now. Kai and I will swim there if you don't let us on this raft." Arik stared out his father. Morgan chuckled slightly. "What's funny?"

"Just the way you lay down the law son, reminds me of your mother. And the way Kai sees the good in everyone reminds me of myself." Morgan hung his head and went quiet. Arik knew he was thinking about Hugo. And Vivienne. And Terra.

As the veil of darkness cloaked the sea, Arik and his dad began to lower the raft into the water. The starlight reflected off the black liquid like a thousand diamonds had fallen from a ring and scattered into the abyss. Ribbons of white light rolled down from the porcelain moon and layered the peaks of the black marzipan water in soft white icing. Everything seemed calm and tranquil. Arik looked over at his dad who was twisting his wedding ring round and round despondently.

"She's going to be okay, Dad." He tried to reassure his father but hardly even convinced himself. "Where's Kai?"

"I'm here!" Kai beamed as he stepped through the broken doorway with a lunchbox in one hand and Morgan's baseball bat in the other.

"What's the bat for?" Arik enquired.

"I told him to fetch me it. It's for protection." Morgan interjected. Arik and Kai glanced at each other but said nothing. "Right, Kai, you first." Morgan grabbed Kai beneath his skinny arms and placed him down on the raft. Arik followed, swinging his legs down first then carefully lowering himself from the deck. Morgan passed down the baseball bat, which Arik took tentatively, then boarded the raft in a similar fashion to how Arik had. Morgan picked up the plank that he had sort of made into an oar and pushed it against one of the deck pillars. They began to drift away from their home. All three were silent. It had been made clear that nobody was to talk unless in case of an emergency. Kai was sitting down with his little lunchbox grinning though. Arik supposed he was excited to be leaving the house for the first time and didn't quite understand the sheer significance and danger of the quest they were embarking on. Morgan was terrified. Although he wasn't showing it, Arik could feel the fear emanating from him. Arik himself was neither excited nor afraid. He was simply determined; determined to get back the family that was stolen from him.

They drifted further away from home and closer to The Mainland. Most of the way they were able to glide stealthily beneath the algae-smothered timber of other stilt houses. They weaved in and out of soggy posts and ducked below rotting steps that creaked and echoed in the hollow space beneath a house. Soon enough the houses dissipated and there was nothing left between them and The Mainland but sea. As they edged closer, they began to make out searchlights scanning the sea. Arik cursed under his breath.

"Shhh!" Morgan hushed him.

"You didn't say there would be searchlights!" Arik whispered again but louder. Morgan spun round and shot Arik a look that warned him to shut his mouth. Then Kai spoke, not whispered, spoke.

"Dad, we don't need to hide from the Femaestus. Not with Arik's bracelet."

"Will you please just shut up, the pair of you, you'll get us all killed." Morgan growled through gritted teeth. "I'm going to steer us more over that way where there seems to be less lights on the water." Morgan was whispering again. Arik looked out to where his dad was pointing when he remembered the cove Tempestas had taken him to. It was in the opposite direction.

"Dad, no, we have to go the other way." He suddenly blurted out.

"Now's not the time for ridiculous suggestions, Arik."

"No seriously, that way there's a cove which I've been to and it's in a cliff so steep the humans don't bother to patrol it." As soon as Arik heard himself say 'the humans' out loud, he knew his dad wasn't going to take him seriously. Morgan looked at him disappointedly and began paddling the raft in the opposite direction to what Arik had suggested. Morgan was seldom pushing the oar in the water, ensuring a minimum speed to allow time for him to assess the best route through the searchlights. His navigation was superb as they glided between the large discs of light skimming the water's surface. The edge of The Mainland was now faintly visible and, with proper eye adjustment, guard towers that housed the source of the lights could be seen distributed along the shoreline. The raft shifted and swayed on the wobbly water but not enough to cause imbalance. The three of them remained perfectly still as they edged closer and closer to The Mainland. That was until a distant boom sounded far away from them, followed by a whizzing noise which whistled past Arik's ear and zipped into the water behind them. Arik and Morgan ducked while Kai hid behind his lunchbox. Distant echoes of men shouting just about reached their ears. Another two bangs rang out also trailed by streamline breaks in the water around them. Gunshots. They had been spotted. It hadn't mattered that they had stayed in the darkness, they could still be seen.   "We need to jump!" Arik yelled.

"No! Nobody jumps! We have more chance of rowing as fast as possible to a cave or something than we do jumping!" Morgan shouted back at him as the gunshots increased in frequency and accuracy. One hit the raft. Arik jumped in. Kai followed.

"Boys, get out of there now! The Femaestus!" Morgan bellowed. The two boys resurfaced from their jump. Arik naturally slipped himself between Kai and the direction the bullets were coming from.

"Dad, come on!" Arik pleaded with his father. "You have to trust me."

"Dad you're being shot at, get in!!" cried Kai, as bullets began to ricochet off the raft that was drifting away from them. Pieces of wood splintered up into the air right by Morgan's feet. Kai screamed again. "Dad, please jump in, we'll be safe!"

"No!"

"Dad!"

"Boys! Behind you!" The boys turned in the water to see four beautiful faces shrouded by flat wet hair staring back at them. One of them was Tempestas. Arik could have cried with relief but there was no time. Arik spun back round in the water to see his dad, now armed with his baseball bat, run to the edge of the raft and launch himself into the water. As he did so, his body began to convulse and jerk in the air. It wasn't until he smacked against the water face down and did not move that Arik realised it was because he had been shot. Arik felt his heart stop for a few moments. He pushed himself over to his dad's still, floating body. Three dark red holes could be seen where the bullets had perforated his coat and entered his back. Arik sniffed as he wiped his face. The water around him began to warm as the heat from his father's fresh blood encased his body. Time seemed to stand still. All sounds reduced to muffled rumblings in the back of Arik's mind somewhere. He pushed his shaky arms up through the water and grasped his dad's coarse jacket. He pulled down on one side to turn his father over onto his back. His stone-white face gleamed with salty water and his empty eyes reflected the void of the night sky above. A smooth line of crimson leaked from his lips and trickled down into the water.

"Dad…" Arik whispered, brokenly, as he sunk his brow into Morgan's limp torso and sobbed.

Then another gunshot hit the water nearby and Arik's senses came flooding back to him. He turned and fled back to his brother and the girls.

"Let's go," he instructed. As they hooked themselves onto the girls, Kai was wailing, not screaming, but yearning for his Daddy.

Air gushed welcomingly into Arik's lungs as they finally broke the water's surface; the saltiness of the water caused him to gag slightly. After inhaling through his nose a couple of times Arik began to realise that it probably wasn't just the salty water making him feel sick; a putrid, rotting, mouldy smell crawled the walls of his nostrils and climbed right into the back of his throat. The hostile stench invaded his body right down to his stomach and forced him to retch again. He rubbed his face with the back of his hands and peered out. As his sore eyes adjusted to the gloominess, he was able to make out that they were in the cave Tempestas and he had been in just over a day ago. Arik thought about how much his life had changed in that small space of time. The last time he was in the cave he had a father, a mother, a baby sister and his brother. Now he wasn't sure about any of those things except Kai. The last time he was in the cave he was the happiest he'd ever been in his life. His heart was full of love and hope and everything in his little life was perfect. The last time he was in the cave. If only he could rewind the past 24 hours, he thought. Could he have stopped it all from happening? The offensive odour that oozed out of the cave caused him to heave again and Kai, who had just been standing next to him on the rock clenching his hand, simultaneously vomited into the pool in front of them. The Femaestus, with grimaces slapped onto their faces, gusted themselves backwards with one swift flick of a tail to avoid the floating stomach contents. Arik's stomach had finally settled enough for him to say something.

"What's that smell?" he questioned the girls. None responded verbally, but Tempestas raised a shaky hand from the water and pointed somewhere beyond where Arik and Kai were stood. Kai looked up at his brother, wide eyed with worry. His grip on Arik's hand tightened. Arik himself was chilled to the bone, with both fear and cold, but Kai needed him to be strong. So, Arik began to turn around. At first he was met with only more darkness. His eyes adjusted slightly but not quite enough. He took a step forward, then another. The slimy floor sucked at his feet and his shoes were skidding. Soon he was more sliding than stepping. He slowed down, tried to re-establish strong footing. But it was no use. His shoes swiped across the algae covered stone and he crashed down – but he did not hit the floor. In fact, he was met with soft body-like cushioning. The smell was even worse down here among whatever it was. He began to feel around. Suddenly Arik's hand met another hand. A cold, stiff hand with no pulse. He yelped. He tried to scramble to his feet but they were slipping on something too. Tails! Heavy winding tails lay over his legs like twisting vines. Arik jerked and turned and eventually pulled himself up and dived out of the pile of bodies. Dead bodies. Dead Femaestus. A saturated graveyard of fishy lifeless girls slept silently at the back of the cave.

"Who did this?" Arik whispered.

"We don't know but each day we come back and there are more. I still haven't seen any humans down here. I get the feeling it's something much worse." Arik didn't believe that there could be anything worse than humans but he understood and trusted Tempestas. Still, if it wasn't the humans hunting down and bringing dead Femaestus to the cave...what was it?

As the sun rose Arik and Kai said goodbye to the girls. Arik kissed Tempestas on her soft salty lips. It would have been the perfect goodbye if Kai hadn't started giggling behind him. Arik wasn't angry at him but he spun round and grabbed him firmly by the wrist nevertheless to avoid further embarrassment in front of Tempestas.

"Come on, we have to get going," he instructed his little brother. They started to head to the side of cave when Kai snatched his hand away and went running back. He had forgotten his lunchbox. Arik just shook his head and told him to get a move on; time was passing quickly and Arik wasn't sure how much of it his mum and sister had left.

At the side of the cave was a narrow slit just wide enough for the two boys to squeeze through and shuffle onto a thin ledge that stuck out about three feet above the water. Arik stood as far back as he could, his heels dangling an inch over the edge, in order to try to analyse the best route for their ascent. It wasn't far but the incline was almost vertical. Arik surveyed every protruding rock, every bulbous clump of weeds and every concave potential foot hole. He was thinking like his father and it wasn't long until he could see the best route.

"Kai, you go first. I'm going to stand here and direct you but you have to do EXACTLY as I say – do you hear me?" Kai nodded and shuffled his feet nervously. He hung his head and gazed at his tiny red lunchbox. "You know you're not going to be able to get that up there with you, right?" Kai flung his head back up to glare at his brother. Arik knew that look.

"Yes I can!" Kai yelled defiantly. Arik sighed and rolled his eyes. He didn't have time for Kai to start throwing a tantrum. He was about to explode into a rage at his little brother who clearly did not understand the awfulness or urgency of their situation when something inside him suddenly stopped him from doing so. Arik took a step back and looked at Kai through his father's eyes and began assessing how his dad would have handled the situation. That's when he decided to approach it differently.

"Tell you what Kai, why don't we eat what you've brought with you now then we won't need to take the lunchbox? How does that sound?" Arik smiled and placed a hand on Kai's shoulder just as Morgan would have done. But Kai's response was not what Arik had expected.

"Sounds impossible. Because it's not food." Kai's reply was suspicious and concerned Arik.

"What's in the lunchbox, Kai?"

■ ■

"Noth-"

"Don't! Don't, say 'nothing'." Arik exhaled slowly but intensely and shoved his hands in his greasy black hair, yanking on it slightly. He was trying so hard to remain calm with his incessantly aggravating little brother. "Just show me," he finally whispered. The technique of Arik remaining calm seemed to work as Kai proceeded to do as he was told. He flicked his little fingers beneath the miniature yellow latches either side of the box and opened it. Arik peered in to find Kai had not brought food supplies, as he had assumed all along, but instead in the box rested two bracelets, one large and one small, both made out of tiny shells of multiple pastel colours.

"I made them for Mum and Terra. I've been making them for ages. I thought if I bring them it would help get them home safely." Kai shut his eyes, as if ashamed. Arik's heart bubbled to the brim with an overwhelming sense of love.

"This is beautiful, Kai," he reassured his sweet little sibling, "here, it looks just like my one," Arik slid his bracelet off and lay it down between the two Kai had made to show him what an excellent job he'd done of making the bracelets similar to his one, "now let's go get them before it's too late, yeah?" Arik ruffled Kai's tuft of hair. He smiled. He forgot where he was. He stepped back and plummeted into the sea.

"Arik!" Kai screeched as a few loose rocks also tumbled into the sea below. Kai held his breath as he scanned the water. He had already lost nearly all his family, he couldn't lose Arik too. He held his breath as his eyes brimmed with tears. "Please, Arik. Please." Kai whimpered to himself. After what seemed like a lifetime, Kai heard his brother emerge from the water with an almighty gasp. He located him and called to him.

"Arik! Catch!"

"No, Kai, wait! Don't throw me the bracelet! I can't get back up from here, I'll have to swim back round to the front of the cave. You're still within reaching distance of the girls so you still need the bracelet."

"But I have two more bracelets!" Kai broke into tears. He was terrified. Fear consumed him just as viciously as the Femaestus would if he threw Arik that bracelet and waited on the ledge alone. But he didn't care about himself; he desperately wanted his brother to be ok so, without a second thought, he tossed a bracelet into the water… but he had already swum out of sight.

As Arik neared the front of the cave, just inches from the entrance, an overwhelming sense of another presence nearby washed over him. He paused and trod the water for a few seconds. He glared down trying to penetrate the water with his vision but he couldn't see anything below other than his own legs kicking. He concluded that whatever it was must be behind him. Gradually, as if not to startle whatever was watching him, he twisted his body round. There, bobbing about thirty feet away in the water, was Tempestas. A mixture of the distance and the salty water in his eyes meant he could barely see her face properly but he knew it was her. He thrust a skinny wet arm out of the water and waved frantically at his love.

"Tempestas, come give me a boost up into the cave!" He yelled as his smile pushed his ears back on his head. Suddenly, Tempestas ducked below the water as quick as the fastest bolt of lightning – barely even noticeable. Arik thought it a bit odd. He had never seen her move that fast and she didn't even shout anything back. Before long, a slim dome-shaped wave had emerged from the water and was tearing towards him at high speed. Within seconds it reached him and as he glanced down into the water this time, his legs weren't alone. A rotten grey face stared back at him. Its skin was loose and full of holes and tears as if it had been sprayed with acid. Inside its oversized jaw rested rows of agitated jagged teeth that sat like lions lying in wait for their prey. Its hair was a few strands of matted string wrapping round her head tangling round her throat. But it was the eyes that terrified Arik most. Though mostly black and soulless, it was the tiny hint of fire and blood that shone through the void that absorbed his fear as if it were breakfast. Suddenly it's spiny hands grasped Arik's legs and yanked him so his face ducked beneath the water. It drew back one hand and jabbed a sharp metal-like finger into Arik's thigh, piercing his muscle and releasing blood. Arik tried to scream but all that came out was a cry muffled by bubbles and his lungs took on some water. The thing in front of him revealed a tongue like that of a lizard, which began soaking up the blood in the water and Arik knew he didn't have long before she would drag him down and finish him off. Despite this, Arik knew that deep down it was still Tempestas and he didn't want to hurt her even if he could. That's when Arik realised that what he needed to do was not hurt her but love her. One kiss gives a sailor a moment of insanity but Arik prayed right now it would give a Femaestus a moment of clarity. Leaving her finger stuck in his thigh on one side and thrusting her arm away on the other, he forced his way towards the horrifically ugly beast in front of him and kissed its gaping, flesh-strewn jaw.

The dullness of the colours that surrounded them blossomed into golds and reds and were underpinned by a metallic green. The cavernous holes that previously layered Tempestas' skin morphed back together before Arik's very eyes as if being rapidly cross-stitched by an invisible needle. Her orthogonal joints began to soften and her skin tightened smoothly round her bones, cushioning and caressing them. Her previously extensive jaw shrivelled to a perfect pair of pout lips and her grey slate eyes flooded with a deep lily-pad green. While she took a moment to reanimate, Arik propelled himself to the surface with one strong push. He took a deep gulp of air. As he did so, a searing pain struck through his other thigh and he was again yanked below the surface. Amongst the bubbles and the foam and the flapping and the kicking and the chaos, Arik became quickly aware that Tempestas had sliced into his other thigh and dragged him back down. While her beauty beamed brightly on the outside, it was just a façade. Arik did not have the bracelet and thus Tempestas did not have control over herself. Thinking quickly, Arik felt behind him in the water. He knew he was at the base of the cave still. His hands soon met some rocks. None would come loose. His hands kept slipping over them. His lungs cried out for oxygen. His thighs throbbed and burned and lost all strength. His kicking was becoming weak and his ability to grasp a rock was proving even less successful. Tempestas moved her face in closer to his and emitted what sounded like an underwater war cry. Her mouth remained open as the sound ceased. She pushed in even closer until her teeth where inches away from Arik's neck. Suddenly her head flung backwards and she dropped downwards. As she descended, Arik could see a boulder sitting between her shoulder blades and her tail, sinking her into the depths below him. Arik scrambled up to the surface, hauling himself up the rocks and into the cave. He spluttered mouthfuls of water into his hands and wiped his eyes. Standing next to him, peering down at the water with shaky outstretched hands, was Kai.

■■■

20

The day, when Penelope had to go back to work, came around all too fast. She splashed her face with cool water, lifted her head and smoothed back her hair as she did every morning before work. Although today wasn't going to be like every other day, she told herself. Today would be the day she would do something about Grace. But what exactly was it she was going to do? And *how* was she going to do whatever it was? If she could do something to Grace, then who else might take her place? Would it ever end? Questions flooded Penelope's brain as she let the cool water smother her hands. Quickly, she snapped shut the tap. While she didn't exactly have a plan, Penelope knew in her heart that she would do all it took to bring down Grace.

Sam was sleeping peacefully in the front room and Penelope decided not to wake him; he needed all the rest he could get to heal. She picked up her handbag, slid her keys briskly off the side and headed for the door. Not far down the hallway was the lift. She pressed the flat silver triangle with the glowing green outline and waited for it. The wait seemed longer than usual. For some reason, Penelope's heart beat faster with every electronic orange floor number increment that signalled above the doors. Suddenly the lift dinged and Penelope's entire body spasmed with fright. Her breath swooped out of her lungs in a hurried gasp as she drew her hand swiftly to her chest. She shook her head as the doors opened. She needed to relax. She couldn't enter S.T.A.B. in this trembling state. She stepped inside the mirrored lift which reflected dozens of small white lights back at her. She found these quite calming. Penelope took a deep breath as the doors slid shut silently and the lift began its soundless descent. In the seconds it took the lift to reach the ground floor, Penelope had managed to gain control over her frenetic breathing. The lift snuggled into the ground floor gently and a second or two passed before the doors began to slide open again. As they did, they revealed a person on the other side waiting to enter. The svelte black figure and opaque square sunglasses resting on a sullen white face was all too familiar to Penelope. The tempo of her pulse shot back up, playing a painful cadence in her ears as beads of sweat formed on her scalp. Her heart drummed against her chest and her skin tightened all over as if her body was about emit some belligerent war cry. It was Grace. Here, in the lobby of her building, waiting to crawl into the lift and climb, presumably, up to Penelope's flat, was the animal she had been planning on hunting all morning. Grace raised her head as a slim smile sliced open her face. Penelope glanced around only to find herself surrounded by eight or so other Grace's in the lifts mirrored walls. She had to get out the lift and prevent Grace from entering. Without hesitation, Penelope broadened her mouth into a teeth-bearing beam and began to step hurriedly out of the lift. She strode straight past Grace until Grace had to have her back to the lift to face Penelope; that's when Penelope spoke.

"Grace! Sorry, I didn't expect that to be you there. How are you? What brings you here?" Grace's thin sharp smile was a forced one. It was clearly hiding the angst she felt for having bumped into Penelope at the bottom of the lift rather than in her apartment. For a few seconds, Penelope was sure she almost heard frustration in Grace's usually emotionless voice.

"Penelope, I do apologise. I was simply doing rounds to remind everyone S.T.A.B. was open again today in case the emails hadn't been received. Lots of equipment hasn't been working properly since the explosion..." Penelope had never felt so sure that someone was lying before. Even with Grace's persuasive tone, convincing posture and influencing gesticulations, it was not enough to hide the truth from Penelope. Grace had been on her way to Penelope's apartment to find signs of Sam.

"Indeed!" Penelope smiled, "I received your email, so I guess we can head to work now?"

"I guess we can." Grace's annoyance was so strong in the air now that Penelope could almost taste it. Penelope headed for the exit. Grace took one last glance at the lift before following Penelope out of the apartment building.

Penelope and Grace walked down the street towards S.T.A.B. side by side – as if they were two best friends going for a casual stroll. Except neither of them spoke. Penelope decided to stay quiet through fear of giving something away about Sam; she suspected Grace had the same idea. Not only that, but Penelope was also not sure she could control what she might say to Grace. She despised her. Every click-clack of Grace's heels against the pavement irritated Penelope and grated against her temper. Every swish and flick of silky black hair, that whipped the outskirts of Penelope's peripheral vision, felt like it was physically poking her repeatedly. Every time she thought about the rotten stumps that remained of Sam's legs she felt like pouncing on Grace and throttling her. She had to get away from her. Although the walk to S.T.A.B. was short, she could not bear completing it with Grace by her side.

"I just have to go to the shop. Grab some lunch." Penelope dropped her words bluntly.

"Okay," Grace smiled falsely, "I'll catch up with you at work." With that, Grace twisted on her heel and continued clacking down the street towards the disturbing S.T.A.B. building. Penelope immediately crossed the road without looking. You barely had to check when crossing the roads anymore. Only a few cars remained on The Mainland and those were reserved for certain people. Penelope wondered if Grace was one of those certain people. Then she shook her head. She had to forget about Grace for a moment and regain control of her emotions. Taking down Grace was going to take brains, not uncontrolled anger. Something in the shop window caught Penelope's eye. It was a poster offering a discount on Chocolate Fake. Penelope thought of Sam, smiled to herself then walked into the shop.

21

Arik howled like a wolf crying to the moon. His heart hurt so much it was as though the very blood pumping through it was laced with poison. He threw a tightly clenched fist into the cave floor repeatedly until no skin, and almost no tissue, remained on his knuckles, before sinking his face into his own warm blood, pressing it against the cool stone and sobbing vocally into the floor. Kai crouched down next to him and tentatively reached out his hand to place on his brother's shoulder. Arik immediately flung it away.

"Don't touch me!" he cried. His breathing was becoming extreme and he began to retch. Kai tried once more to put his hand on his brother's shoulder. This time, he didn't reject it. Gently, Kai rolled his traumatised brother over and begun to hush him softly. He scrambled around for something to bandage Arik's wounds with, all the while hushing his big brother to help him slow his breathing. Arik soon became calmer and placed his uninjured hand over his eyes as his quivering jaw still showed signs of sadness, his mouth curved down into a mournful half circle, displaying his bottom teeth. Kai didn't speak. Instead he silently began tearing off strips of his already fraying vest and wrapping them around Arik's knuckles before moving onto the holes in his thighs. Arik didn't flinch once. At one point Kai even slipped and prodded one of Arik's thigh wounds but Arik was stuck in a stasis that bound him within his own mind and cut off physical connection. Kai was relieved in a way as he was sure his brother would have killed him by now if not. But then Kai remembered the mission. Arik couldn't remain stuck like this. He had to snap out of it and snap out of it fast. Kai began to shake his brother.

"Arik, Arik? Arik, we must go get mum, remember? And little Terra? Arik, they need us. Arik, what about Dad? If you give up now that means he died for nothing. Look Arik, I'm sorry. I'm so sorry but Dad needed you and now Mum and Terra need you and I can't do this alone. I need you. Arik please. I did the right thing. We need you. I saved you because Mum and Terra need you but also because I love you." Kai burst into a flood of tears. He dragged his knees up to his chest, wrapped his arms around his legs and bawled deeply into his lap. He hadn't even had a chance to cry since Morgan died. It was like oceans of emotion just suddenly flooded his tiny body, overflowed and came spewing out. He missed his daddy. He missed his mummy. He missed his sister. And now, although he was right there physically, he was missing his brother. As he sat there and cried miserably into his legs, two arms suddenly embraced him, shrouding him with warmth and affection.

"Dad?" he sniffed as he lifted his head. There, holding him tight, was Arik. The two smiled.

"I may not be Dad," Arik whispered, "but I will *always* be here for you." They continued their hug for a moment before Arik pulled away. "We have to get moving, Kai." The two brothers wiped their wet, tear-soaked faces with the back of their sleeves and cleared the snot from their noses onto their tops. Arik shook his head like a dog to try and dry his salty hair off and Kai wiped the blood from Arik's wounds off his hands onto his clothes. "Let's go." Arik ushered Kai in front of him. As he bent down to pick up the bag, and while Kai wasn't looking, Arik took one last look into the water. He felt a pang in his heart and a sickness in his stomach. Then he turned and followed Kai back to the side of the cave.

Back out on the ledge, where Arik had fallen in previously, sat Kai's open lunch box. As they neared it, Arik noticed something that filled him with dread. Only two bracelets remained in the lunchbox and, although all three had been nearly identical, Arik could tell that neither of them were the true bracelet. Kai must have thrown him the actual bracelet despite Arik's plea for him not to. In some vain hope of still having protection, Arik grabbed the two bracelets and put one on himself and the other on Kai, before quickly getting to work clambering up the cliff face. Kai seemed to navigate the rocks with ease, despite the almost vertical 9655gradient and the hot sun melting their backs all the while. His lightweight and nimble body allowed him to scale the cliff face like a streamline monkey. While Arik was a little slower, eventually they both hauled themselves over the top edge and stood up... on The Mainland. Arik pulled Kai a few steps away from the sheer drop behind them. As he did so, he felt something tickling his toes where he still had his old worn out sandals on. He looked down to see juicy green ribbons of grass curling up and stroking his feet. Kai looked down and giggled.

"Look, Arik! It's grass!" exclaimed Kai. They laughed together for a few minutes as they enjoyed the sensation of grass against their feet for the first time. For a brief moment, Arik forgot about all the bad things; as the warm sun caramelised his face, the cool grass moistened his toes and the echo of his brother's laughter tickled his ears. The air up here was dense, burning and barely breathable, quite different to the cool sea air the boys were use to. It was a surreal feeling, standing on The Mainland. But Arik had a family to save and soon forced himself from his blissful moment to begin surveying the area for threats as well as ideas on where to go next.

From where the boys stood, all Arik could see was a lookout tower, a wall, a hedge and a thin strip of grass between them. A noise began to rumble quietly in the distance. It sounded to Arik like a boat but it was coming from further in The Mainland. It must have been something else with an engine – a car, perhaps? Soon, Arik could make out the top of what he knew was a car, from books he had read, heading across the land in front of them. It wasn't coming towards them, instead it was heading for the looming wooden tower that stood tall in the grass beyond them. Arik guessed these were the soldiers coming to man it for the day.

"Do you reckon those are the ones that shot Dad?" Kai whimpered from down by Arik's side. Arik looked down at Kai and sighed. He took his little hand firmly. "Come on," he said.

The two sprinted for the hedgerow that ran down the side of the grass and the tower, crouching all the while. Arik's thighs throbbed. A lunging run was already a difficult workout without wounded thighs and a new terrain to adjust to. Arik slumped down once they reached the other side of the bush. Kai pulled a face. "Are you okay?"

"I'm fine," breathed Arik, "I just need to take a moment." He controlled his breathing well. With his eyes shut, he inhaled the fresh woody scent of the bush behind him then exhaled his hot breath into the warm air. He opened his eyes. The sight of the colour green enlivened him. "We have to follow this bush all the way down to that wall, Kai. That's where the car came from and that's how we get to the other side of that wall." Arik was whispering slowly to ensure Kai understood. "Keep low." Kai nodded obediently.

The two decided to crawl prone all the way. They couldn't get much flatter than that and there was no way the guards in the tower were going to see them from that angle. Arik dragged his sore thighs along the ground, through pointy stones and piercing sticks and spiky plants. With every pull he could feel his bandages loosening and the agony in his wounds growing. Sweat poured from his scalp and clumped dirt and sand in an uneven paste round his face. Each of his breaths felt so loud to him, especially as the boys passed right under the tower. Arik could hear the guards laughing from down on the ground so could they hear his breathing? No, he was just being paranoid. The fear of getting caught yanked at his nerves while flashbacks of his dad lying face down in the sea recurred in his mind, but he kept going. After what seemed like a lifetime, the two of them squeezed between the bush and the edge of the wall and sat down on the other side.

The boys couldn't believe what they saw beyond the wall. Houses, real brick-built houses, lined the road in front of them. There was a pavement with the odd dry tree sprouting every five or six paces. Behind the terraced houses loomed even taller buildings, made mostly of glass and reaching up into the sky. The sun bounced off one of the windows and blinded Arik for a second. He squinted down the street. At the end was an ugly creamy-grey spherical building with strong metal joists snaking round it. The sight of it made Arik shudder. Suddenly Kai spoke.

"Look, Arik! That shop has Chocolate Fake!" He was pointing eagerly across the road to a small red shop that had its windows covered in posters. The biggest poster of them all boasted a giant wedge of deep brown cake. Arik felt his stomach rumble.

"We can't get any, Kai. They use money here on The Mainland and we don't have any." Kai peered up at his big brother with his doughy puppy eyes.

"Can't we just go take a look? I've never been in a shop before!" As Kai began to plead, Arik became acutely aware that people were beginning to turn and stare at the two of them just standing wide-eyed at the edge of the pavement. Most people were in smart shirts and crease-free skirts and had silky hair and posh sunglasses. Arik peered down at himself and glanced at Kai. Both had dirty black hair, torn shirts and the blood on Arik's make shift bandages was visible from the outside. Both had sand and dirt and sea salt dried and crusted round their little tanned faces and their shabby sandals were thin and fraying. They stood out like sore thumbs. Quickly, Arik grabbed Kai's arm and began lugging him across the road towards the shop.

Inside the shop was cool. The crisp air greeted their hot skin lovingly. There were plenty of aisles in the shop and Arik decided they would walk up and down them, avoiding people, until he came up with a better plan. How had he not thought about this? Kai was quite happy, meandering slowly round the aisles with his jaw on the floor and his eyes the size of saucers. Awe filled him until he almost looked like he was ready to burst. Arik kept his head down and was contemplating their next move when Kai began pointing at something and calling him over. Arik obeyed reluctantly. He had to keep Kai happy. Soon Arik realised it was the Chocolate Fake that Kai had found. Arik surveyed the shelf and smiled to himself as his mouth brimmed with saliva. What he would give to take just one bite. He reached for the box to take a closer look. Suddenly a voice seeped into his ears from over his shoulder – and it wasn't Kai.

"Where did you get that bracelet?" The voice croaked delicately. Arik turned around to see a young, thin woman with sandy hair and lightly freckled cheeks staring at his wrist. Arik glanced at his bracelet, then back at the woman. She looked gaunt and pasty as if life was draining her of energy by the second. Arik thought she seemed innocent enough – but then what did he know about people?

"I, err, made it," he stammered.

"No you didn't," the woman snapped, but not viciously, more desperately, "I know you didn't because I've seen it before, a long time ago." Arik suddenly saw sadness pour from her eyes. Her brow slumped at the edges as she seemed to trail off into a memory inside her own mind. Behind her, at the end of the aisle, Arik noticed an old couple had appeared and were pointing and scrutinising every inch of Kai and his tatty appearance. Arik felt frantic. He fumbled with the flimsy bracelet that clung to his wrist before staring the woman directly in the eye and telling her, "I'll tell you – if you take me and my brother somewhere safe." The woman twisted round to observe Kai before hastily clutching him and Arik by the hands and walking them out of the shop.

"Where are we going? Who is she?" Kai whined as the woman almost dragged them up the street. Kai's little legs were struggling to keep up with her pace.

"We're almost there," the woman replied before Arik even had a chance to respond to his brother. Within minutes they were inside the lobby of one of the gargantuan glass buildings and they halted abruptly at two silver rectangles that ran almost floor to ceiling but with a narrow gap above them containing a row of numbers. The woman pressed a button and the rectangles slid apart. The trio entered. As soon as the doors closed, the woman let out a prolonged sigh. Arik kept quiet and, to his amazement, so did Kai. Arik glanced at his little brother who was ogling at the numbers, that were also inside above the doors, as they took it in turns to light up. Eventually, the light stopped on number 25 and the doors slid open once more. The woman didn't pull the boys this time, but instead wandered out the cubicle and opened another door across the hall. She turned to see the two, wide-eyed frightened little boys still frozen in the lift.

"Well, are you coming in?" Then a look of sympathy washed over her fatigued face and she smiled and said, "I have Chocolate Fake."

The boys slid into the apartment warily. Kai actually nearly skidded over on the shiny tiled floor and grabbed Arik's hand for support – but he didn't let go of it once he caught his balance. Arik felt his tiny sweaty fingers clasping his own sticky hands. He'd done so well. Arik felt his chest swell with pride. He hoped he hadn't put his little brother in danger by taking this chance.

"So, I'm Penelope. Where are you two from? Why do you need a place of safety? And most of all, why do you have that bracelet?" Penelope had crouched down to Kai's level to begin her tender but eager questioning.

"Woah, woah, woah. What's going on over there?" A deeper but equally soft voice boomed gently from around the corner. "Why are you back already? Who's with you?" Penelope straightened back up. She eyed the two scrawny, emaciated and malnourished boys in front of her; with their tight drawn skin like warm plastic wrap sinking in the gaps between their bones. "Go in there, take a seat and meet Sam," she said in almost a whisper, "I'll get you boys some cake."

Kai peered up at Arik for confirmation on what they should do next, so Arik began to stride confidently around the corner with Kai by his side. Everything around them was either white or grey. And clean. Very clean. Arik had never seen so many pristine smooth surfaces, his eyes felt flat looking at them. Around the corner was a vast open room with featureless square windows completely lining the wall on one side, filling the room with bright natural daylight. The windowed wall was broken by a large flat television in the middle and in the centre of the room was… a hospital bed? Arik thought this strange. He didn't know much about houses that weren't shabby stilt ones but he knew that bed didn't belong there. As they moved round further into the room Arik saw that atop the bed was a man. He had a light short bristly beard and mousey thin hair and a kind smile. Arik was so taken aback by his sweet face that he almost didn't notice that he had no legs.

"Where are your legs?" Kai burst out. The man, Sam, emitted at feeble, half-hearted laugh. Arik felt the need to jump in and say something sensible, or even apologise on his brother's behalf, but his curiosity got the better of him. He too wanted to know why this kind looking man had no legs.

"Well, let's just say there are some pretty nasty people out there who tricked me into losing my legs. Gotta be careful here on The Mainland." Sam knew they were not from The Mainland. Arik felt uneasy.

"I thought The Mainland was the safe place? Where all the lucky people live?" Kai's face twisted into a whirlpool of confusion as questions continued to cascade from his mouth. Arik felt irritated by his naivety.

"Don't be silly Kai," he hissed through grated teeth, "The Mainland is obviously where the soldiers came from that took mum and Terra. That's why we're here. You *know* that." Suddenly Penelope appeared from around the corner, brandishing a pair of small white circular plates with a glistening chunk of Chocolate Fake perched atop each one and two tiny silver forks resting on the sides. "Your mum was taken by soldiers?"

"Yes, and our sister!" Kai yelped.

"Why?" Penelope's tone remained endearing. Arik nudged Kai with his elbow; an indication to his brother that he should stop talking. Kai let out a squeak and held his arm while glaring up at Arik with a surly expression. Even though Arik had given Kai the warning not to talk, Arik still remained silent himself. A few awkward moments passed until Penelope gave them a plate of cake each. The sickly smell of the chocolate lulled Arik into a blissful honey coloured trance. Kai was already diving in, so Arik raised his fork and cut himself a small piece. As the rich creamy topping kissed his lips he felt as though the world began to liquify around him. The velvet soft sponge melted into his taste buds as the flavour danced in colourful waves between his teeth, causing his inner cheeks to tingle and buzz. Soon he was cramming in the next mouthful, before finishing the last and his mouth became stodged with the electrifying ecstasy of Chocolate Fake. Even if he wanted to talk now, he physically couldn't.

"Do you boys want some water?" Penelope giggled. Both boys nodded wildly; despite never wanting the cake to end, Arik was getting to the point where he could barely breathe.

The boys finished their cake and washed it down with a whole glass of water each. Arik realised that even the water tasted like divine droplets of heaven had been collected and poured lovingly into a crystal-clear glass. They barely had time to savour the moment when Penelope spoke up again. "So, boys, first of all, tell me your names. Then tell me your story."

"I'm Kai," Arik darted him a stern look. Kai shrugged his shoulders.

"I'm Arik." The words left his lips with great reluctance.

"OK, so, Kai, Arik, tell us. Where are your mum and sister? And why were they taken?"

"First tell us why you have no legs!" Kai shouted at Sam. Then he beamed up at Arik, as if proud of himself that he had got the hang of the idea of bartering for information exchanges.

"Look, we're not here to bring you any harm. In fact, we may be able to help you. The people who took Sam's legs were also soldiers and we are after them too. We might be able to get your mum and sister back, but you need to tell us what's going on." Penelope placed a soft hand on Arik's shoulder as she spoke and he felt his cold heart thaw. He missed his mum. He missed his mum so so much. He shut his eyes for a second and imagined it was his mums hand resting protectively his shoulder. He missed his dad too. He couldn't get his dad back now – but he could do something about getting his mum.

"The soldiers took our mum and our baby sister because she was born with legs. Our dad...he didn't make it here." Arik noticed Penelope's eyes drop to his wrist. He placed his hand over his bracelet. "Dad helped us get so far, this bracelet got us the rest of the way."

"Your sister was born with legs?" Penelope gasped with delight, with hope. Her mind flashed to Travis; how she wished he was here now to receive this unbelievable news. "But that's impossible! Incredible!" Her voice was intensifying in pitch until she realised she had barely listened to the second part of Arik's journey. She looked at the two, almost orphaned, boys with a heaviness returning to her heart.

"How do you mean the bracelet got you the rest of the way?" Penelope's voice splintered with sadness at Arik's sullen story.

"It stops the Femaestus attacking when they are near it. I got it off one that… that I killed. Accidentally."

"It wasn't an accident." Kai mumbled almost inaudibly under his breath. Penelope didn't notice. Her eyes were brimming with tears.

"That Femaestus, the one you got the bracelet from, I put her in the sea about fifteen years ago, wearing that bracelet," Penelope's voice rose to a high-pitched squeak as she clasped one hand over her mouth, "and now it's helping you boys get back to your mum." Arik could hardly swallow the fact that Penelope just simply believed him, and he certainly wasn't sure by this point if Penelope was happy or sad. Neither was Penelope. A nutritiously toxic mix of emotions effervesced within her stomach and gassed her happy heart. Sam reached over from the bed and placed his hand on her back. She felt it calm the chaos inside her, soothe the storm, pacify the pandemonium. The rage of knowing these boys had had their mother and sister taken from them by Grace and her foot soldiers was quelled by the fact the bracelet had saved these delicate souls.

"Right," Penelope cleared her throat and clapped her hands once, "let's go get your mother and sister back."

Penelope summoned the brothers to another room. This one had no windows. A glistening silver shower head jutted out from the wall and Penelope turned it on. Water sprayed from the nozzle and splashed at their toes. She told them to strip off and go inside and have a good wash. The boys followed her orders. While the boys showered Penelope got to work scrubbing their clothes down but it was no use – their t-shirts were in shreds and their shorts were blood stained.

"What am I going to do? How can I dress them?" Penelope flustered, half talking to herself, half asking Sam. "Sam, do you have anything at all?" Sam pulled a face at her. "Sorry," she added quickly.

"Penelope, calm down. What's your plan anyway?" Sam hushed.

"Take the boys, rescue their mum and sister, expose Grace for what she really is and the truth behind S.T.A.B." Sam could see Penelope's mind was made up but he couldn't let her walk herself and those boys to their deaths – or worse. "Penelope, you won't be able to do this. You won't get within an inch of that place without raising eyebrows, not with two young boys with you who have appeared from nowhere. Plus, look at what Grace did to me – imagine what she will do to you. Who's to say their mum is even in S.T.A.B.?" Penelope didn't even look at Sam but instead continued to scramble with scissors and clothes.

"Sam, if there is so much of a chance to make a difference, I'm going to take it. And you can't stop me." She continued cutting and fumbling.

"Fine," Sam sighed, "but at least leave the younger lad here with me. He can't go Penelope." Penelope lowered her arms slowly and rested them in her lap. She looked over to Sam lovingly.

"You're right," she finally agreed to something. At that moment, the two dripping-wet and completely naked boys shuffled into the room.

"All done!" Kai beamed.

"Me too!" Penelope laughed as she threw them both some clothes. For Arik she had found the smallest plain black t-shirt she had and cut the bottoms off some old skinny jeans. She threw Kai a soft and cosy, lilac coloured, oversized jumper that had a small white cartoon cat on the front. The boys wriggled into their new clothes. Kai looked at his brother, then down at himself, then frowned.

"I look like I'm going to bed!" Kai remarked.

"Well, we were thinking that's more along the lines of what you should do…" Sam's tone of voice had that same soothing and reassuring feel as Morgan's had had. Both Kai and Arik felt it and it encouraged Kai to ask his next question calmly and politely, "so what are you saying?"

"We think you should stay here with Sam, Kai. He can look after you until your brother and I get back. There's lots of Chocolate Fake here and some nice boring television." Penelope half-laughed. Kai's face lit up slightly. He turned to Arik. Silence filled the air while everyone waited anxiously for Arik's opinion.

"I think that would be the best idea," Arik exhaled. He even managed a slight smile too as he witnessed the delight in his exhausted brother's face, "you be good for Sam though ok? I promise we won't be gone long." Arik knelt down with his hands on Kai's shoulders. He looked him straight in his large dark eyes. "I love you." With that, Arik snatched his brother in close and squeezed him against his own chest. Every tiny bend and bone of Kai's body folded neatly into Arik's. Arik felt a golden warmth illuminate at every point their bodies connected. Tears welled in his eyes. He didn't want to leave Kai – not one fibre of his tired aching body wanted to leave Kai; the only family he had left right now. But he knew deep in his heart that it was the right thing to do. Even if he never saw him again. If Arik couldn't restore his own family, at least Kai would have a new one here.

22

Penelope and Arik left the building and started down the street toward S.T.A.B. Arik already knew that the ugly round building at the end of the road, that threw the street into darkness with its immense round shadow, was where his mum and sister were harboured. He just felt it in his gut. Soon they passed the little red shop where they had met Penelope just an hour or so earlier. He thought of Kai and a sinking feeling pressed heavily on his chest. He shook his head and reassured himself that he had done the right thing. Penelope was walking so fast even Arik almost struggled to keep up. Before long, they arrived at the entrance of S.T.A.B.

A large glass door outlined in a blackened cream plastic slid open before them - without even touching it. Arik felt uneasy already as if some dark magic lived in this building. He felt that it was the kind of place where things would enter pure but leave painfully poisoned – if they left at all. Arik stepped through the door into the empty cold foyer. Five arched corridor entrances lined the one round wall that encircled them, like ventricles leaving a heart. Arik thought it looked like a maze where only one would lead him in the right direction – and possibly back again. He went to say something to Penelope when he noticed a slim lady in all black attire had seemingly appeared out of nowhere.

"Grace!" Penelope beamed. Arik hadn't known Penelope long, but he already knew that this was not a natural smile for her.

"Penelope, you took your time grabbing some lunch. And who do we have here?" Grace pulled the corner of her glasses and peered over the top of them, eyeing Arik suspiciously. Arik gulped. Penelope felt her heart quicken as sweat started to bubble in her pores.

"This is my nephew. I bumped into my sister in the shop and she desperately needed someone to watch him today, so I said he could come to work with me." Penelope was feigning confidence that she was sure Grace would see right through. Grace continued to look Arik up and down as if scrutinising a bad apple. Penelope knew this was do or die. If Grace didn't believe her, they were both dead. Her heart rammed against her chest in short, sharp, painful pulses.

"I suppose it can do no harm awakening such an impressionable young mind to the ways of the future." Grace finally chirped. To Penelope's surprise, Grace was keen on the idea. The thought of having such an innocent mind to infiltrate and plant ideas in excited her. Little did she know that Arik's mind was far from the empty sponge Grace hoped for.

"So, I'd better check on my patients. Arik, come along now." Penelope began to yank Arik away from Grace's infectious aura. As they scurried off down one of the corridors they heard Grace call, "Certainly, and perhaps later the young boy can come help me out with a few things." Even though Penelope had her back turned to Grace, she could hear her smirking.

Arik scuttled behind Penelope, tracing her steps through a maze of winding corridors. How was he ever going to find his mum in this place? Eventually, the two stopped at a ward of half-dead, zombie-like men who seemed to have become one with their beds.

"Where's mum?" Arik whispered.

"I don't know," replied Penelope, sincerely, "but what I do know is that Grace barely comes here so it gives us time to talk, space to think and the privacy to work out a plan. Now, the only other place I have really been in this whole building is where I found Sam." Arik's eyes widened. He thought of Sam lying in that bed in Penelope's apartment, helpless. He pictured the white sheets that concealed Sam's stumps and shuddered to think what they looked like beneath. A lump formed in his throat as he tried to comprehend what kind of person could do that to somebody else. The kind of person who had his mum and sister – that's who.

"We have to move fast," Arik suddenly panted, "let's go there now!" Penelope pulled a pained face down at Arik as she inhaled deeply and shifted from foot to foot. It was clear she had no idea what else to do. Finally, she responded, "Fine. Let's go."

Penelope and Arik slunk through the corridors speedily like two stealthy snakes. Both allowed their determination to lead them on through the seemingly endless twists and bends of corridor. After what felt like hours of navigating the deathly tunnels, Penelope finally stopped Arik suddenly. In front of them was a heavy steel door with a crimson circle, cut in half by a white line, painted across it. The door with the No Entry sign. The door Penelope had found Sam behind. Arik took a step forward and reached his hand out to open it but Penelope snatched it away. Arik gazed up at Penelope, puzzled.

"What are you doing? Is this where my mum is?"

"Wait!" Penelope ordered. The last time Penelope made a discovery behind this door, an image was printed in her mind that she will never be able to shake from her memory. An image of blood, of helplessness, of suffering and of death. And she didn't even know the man that was at the heart of this image at the time. No, Penelope couldn't let Arik open that door for she was uncertain as to what monstrous scene may greet them on the other side.

"Let me go first," Penelope whispered reassuringly, "just, let me check it's safe." Arik nodded reluctantly. The urgency that zapped through his body and the desperation that electrified his blood was becoming unbearable. He *had* to know if his mother and sister were safe. He *had* to save them. But he also had to listen to Penelope; he wouldn't have gotten this far without her and every decision of hers so far had taken him a step closer to his family.

Penelope placed a shaky hand on the thick cylindrical handle. She pushed it down and the latch mechanism clicked distinctly into the corridor, followed by a brief whoosh of air. Hesitantly, Penelope leaned a shoulder into the door to open it. When the gap was big enough, Penelope slipped her head through and peered round the other side into the room. There was nothing. Well, nothing new anyway. The blood-stained chair that once housed Sam remained perched in the centre of the room, the cold desk was still pushed up into the corner and, worst of all, the glass tubes of pulsating tails throbbed up against the grimy wall. But there was no mother or child. There were no people at all. Suddenly the door fell away from Penelope's face as Arik had barged through under her arm to get a look for himself. A gasp rushed from his mouth as he spied the tubes.

"What are those for?" He squeaked. Penelope couldn't find the words – but she didn't need to. Arik had put the pieces of the puzzle together. He began to picture Sam with a fish tail and he squirmed inside. Then he had another revelation.

"Penelope, Sam wasn't the first one." The words left his mouth in dry cracked syllables.

"What?" Penelope eyed Arik with intrigue.

"Something has been killing the Femaestus. Something below the water. There's a cave – a *graveyard*! It's full of dead girls. They turn grey as stone when they die. It's like a mountain of soft rocks. This must be it. They are making soldiers to eliminate the Femaestus."

"Hmmm, and they're not exactly using volunteers by the looks of it…" Penelope sighed loftily as she thought about Sam back home. "Come on, let's keep moving."

Penelope had no clue where they should go next. She wasn't worried about Grace checking her post – not when she knew that Grace would be particularly busy with other things – but she was becoming increasingly doubtful in her ability to find this young boy's mother and sister. The two of them picked up the pace but remained sharp, stealthy and stuck to the shadows. The part of S.T.A.B. they had been winding their way around was the dark area with the discoloured walls and yellowing linoleum. The evil emitting from the walls in this wing was beginning to suffocate Penelope and, after some time, she felt an overwhelming need to leave. That's when she realised. Penelope had never gone through the entire 'hospitable' area of S.T.A.B., the place she had first gone with the burnt orange and teal walls and black silhouettes of trees. As she considered the size of the building from the outside and the distance she'd actually ventured into the softer area it became clear to her that there was more to that side of the building than she had initially thought. She grabbed Arik's arm and began pulling him back down the corridor towards the link.

"Come, Arik!" Arik viewed the passage ahead of them and recognised it as the way back to reception.

"No! I'm not leaving without my mum and my sister!" he cried. Penelope stopped abruptly, spun round to face Arik and glared at him directly in the eye.

"We are not leaving, Arik. We are going in deeper."

Back at the reception area, the two paused to check first for signs of Grace – or anyone who might be wary of them and thus alert Grace – but the area was empty. The pair scampered across and headed for the passageway directly opposite the one they'd just left. Down this hall, Penelope and Arik assumed a normal and casual walking pace. Penelope had informed Arik that there was more chance of them bumping into Grace in this area and sneaking around would only make them look more suspicious. Instead, the two strode boldly and slowly down the length of the warm rust-coloured corridor, Arik peeking into wards now and again. The colours of the corridor began to drain from the walls as they moved further down. The deep orange gradually faded to a mustard yellow before washing out into a cloudy cream and eventually bursting into a clinical white. The lighter the walls became, the darker the ball of anxiety in Penelope's stomach grew. The gentle gusts of their breaths and the soft patter of their footsteps were drowned by the buzzing of the bright lights overhead. Soon, doors stopped appearing either side of them and instead the corridor came to a close, with one set of frosted glass double doors in front straight ahead. Arik took a deep breath in as Penelope reached for the bar on the door to open it. She gave it a pull. It didn't budge. She pulled again. Nothing. She tried again and again and again.

127

"It's locked," she exhaled with frustration, "of course it's locked." She leaned back against the glass.

"Let's break the glass," Arik suggested.

"No, it's too tough, we'd never even crack it. Besides, it'll draw too much attention." Arik began to feel frustrated. He didn't care about attention. If his mother was the other side of that locked door then they had to break it down. As desperate and irritated as he felt, he once again paused and waited for Penelope's suggestion. Patience. It's what his dad would have reminded him of. Penelope slumped to the floor, her back still against the cool glass and her head in her hands. Her brain rattled around her skull, empty of ideas. She raised her head to check on Arik. As she did so, a glimpse of something red on the wall behind him caught her eye. Fire alarm.

"Arik, move aside," Arik jumped out the way as Penelope launched herself at the small red box and flung the switch down to the floor. The deafening wail of a siren curdled in Arik's ears. Red flashing lights rolled around the walls and further down the corridor some sprinklers had activated. Penelope yanked Arik back down the corridor slightly to the first side door. The two bundled inside what seemed like a broom closet.

"How is this going to work?" Arik hissed loud enough to be heard over the sirens. Penelope wasn't even sure herself yet, but as she strained to look through the crack in the door she could see the double doors had been opened. People were leaving sporadically but even the longest gap between two people exiting wasn't enough time for the slow heavy door to shut fully behind them. Penelope would just have to take a chance on who she thought was the last person to leave.

"Now!" she suddenly exclaimed as she burst through the broom closet door and bolted for the glass ones. The tips of her fingers clasped the silver bar inches from the door shutting and she managed to stabilise her grip and hold it open. Arik shuffled through quickly and Penelope ducked in after him.

"Woah, what is this place?" Arik exclaimed as his eyes widened to try to absorb everything before him. In front of Arik was a silver railing – and beyond that was the greatest circular room he'd ever seen with a drop below of about 4 floors. The open void reached right up about another 4 floors above him. In the centre, a marble white column glittered up through an enormous turquoise pool until it reached the ceiling. The one tiny thing that suggested anything natural in this room was the base of the column which was greened slightly where it met the water but mostly it oozed artificial grandeur. Lining the inner sphere on every level were machines and doors and computers and chairs. Platforms extended at random into the expanse beyond. Arik noticed some of these platforms had the familiar greenish coloured tubes fixed on them that had contained fish tails back in the other room. Some had chairs on like the one Sam was found in, but these were not infected and blood-stained. These chairs were metallic silver at the base with pure white cushioning on top to match the bluish-silver and white colour theme that masked the entire place. A slight movement, far down below on the floor of the open area, caught Arik's attention. It wasn't the water. That sat very still and almost unmoving at the base of the column. Arik could barely see from so far up but he was sure he could make out a person lying on a bed with spotlights invading them from all angles. The person moved again.

"Mum!" Arik yelled. Suddenly he began searching for stairs or some other means of getting down.

"Here!" Penelope called. Between each section round the sphere were stairs leading to the unit below. The pair climbed frantically down endless flights before reaching the floor that made up the bottom of the sphere. Arik launched himself over the railing and sprinted to his mum.

"Mum!" he cried again as he reached her. He flopped his head into her warm chest and sobbed tears of relief.

"Arik," Vivienne responded, weak but equally as overjoyed, "what are you doing here, you shouldn't be here, this is not a safe place."

"I know," Arik choked, exasperated, "that's why I'm here to get you and Terra out. Where is Terra?"

"She's just over there in that cube," Vivienne spat the word 'cube' from her dry mouth, "where's your father?" Arik's eyes dropped to the floor as more salty tears exploded from his eyes and saturated his mother's chest. Vivienne's face shifted into jelly as her lips wobbled and her eyebrows sagged down at the edges. But she did not cry. "And Kai?" she stammered.

"He's safe," Arik assured her through a cracked voice.

"We have to move," Penelope interrupted the reunion with sense and panic. Arik slipped his skinny hands through the shackles that bound his mother to the bed and began fumbling with the heavy leather. Once the first one snapped open, it revealed damp wrinkled skin beneath that was mottled purple and blue. Then Arik noticed the holes in the backs of his mother's hands. A dark rage coursed from his heart, through his veins and out to his fingertips where he clenched his white knuckles into fists.

"Arik, hurry!" Penelope shook him from his stasis of anger and protectiveness and he swiftly darted round the other side of the bed to work on the other binding. Meanwhile, Penelope had removed Terra from her cube with such tenderness that Terra remained silent as she cuddled into the warmth of Penelope. Once the second manacle came loose, Vivienne hauled herself from the icy slab. As she did so, the gown she was wearing came apart slightly at the side and Arik caught a flash of crimson encircled by black smudges on her stomach. The dark rage returned as he wondered what torturous experiments his mother had been put through in the time she'd been in S.T.A.B. Wild great fear, swirled with anger and vengefulness, brewed hot and steaming in his stomach, cooled only slightly by the sadness he felt as he watched his weak and frail mother in front of him. Arik strode round the bed to give his mother some support when a smug voice cackled from behind them.

"Leaving so soon?"

Arik edged round slowly to find a smirking Grace standing behind them, leaning against a wall with one foot crossed over the other. So casual, as if nothing serious was going on. She leaned there like a teacher waiting for a class to calm down. This vexed Arik further. She was dressed in her usual deathly attire; a tight black pencil skirt that cut into her thin waist, a dark shirt shielded by a velvet buttoned blazer, towering midnight heels and her overly-shiny thick rimmed glasses to match her overly-shiny hair. Arik wondered if blood would show on such dark and shadowy clothing.

"I'm taking my mum and my sister away from here," Arik informed her, with bravery and boldness bellowing from his chest. Grace let out a patronising laugh that increased in pitch towards the end before falling into a sigh.

"I don't think so," she smiled smugly, and with that, four burly soldiers armed with some type of bulky gun each, emerged from the medical-blue walls behind her. Penelope turned her back to them instinctively in a bid to shield Terra; Arik stepped in front of his mum. His pulse quickened as the dark, bold vengefulness that ravaged his soul earlier faded into a lacklustre puddle of panic in the pit of his churning stomach. A helpless situation. Of course Grace wouldn't have left such precious property like his mother and sister alone – even during a fire alarm. Arik felt a fool and his foolishness had now put everyone in danger. His father wouldn't have made such a mistake. "Oh don't worry," Grace chuckled as she observed the way Arik and Penelope got protective, "I won't be hurting *those* two." She gestured in an endearing way toward Vivienne and the baby that made Arik sick. Grace continued to mumble on about being kind enough to let them step out of the way and other such nonsense, but Arik had stopped listening. Instead, his attention had been diverted to the pool in the centre of the room. It was no longer still and calm as it had been when they first entered. The seemingly shallow pool began to sway and froth at it's semi-circular mouth, depth and current causing a choppy and jagged surface of silent yet extravagant waves to lap at the edges and stretch up against the central column. The turquoise water darkened quickly and, before Arik could hardly comprehend what was happening, the gargantuan beastly tail of a Femaestus carved through the water and snapped across the room with unfathomable speed. There was no time to react. The tail soared through the air, coming up behind Grace and her four soldiers, and wiped them out from behind, slamming the fearful five into the glistening grey wall. Penelope, Arik, Vivienne and even little Terra all watched, mouths dangling open and eyes agog, as the magnificent glossy tail shimmered under the artificial lights. Soon it began to retract, with less speed, and return to the opening of the pool. "Let's go!" Penelope yelled suddenly. They began to turn for the stairs when Arik halted.

"Wait," he whispered audibly. The two women stopped as they witnessed Arik beginning to walk towards the central pool.

"Arik!" hissed his mother. Arik casually hushed her with a dampening hand gesture behind his back as he continued to advance towards the pool. He approached the low, cold, stone ring that encircled the pool and peered over the top. Something began to emerge from the water, gradually. As it popped out into the air it became clear to Arik that it was his bracelet, clutching it was a spindly but smooth hand wrapped in gleaming milky skin. As the bracelet was pushed further from the surface of the water, and the hand lifted, it revealed an equally pale arm which eventually led to a sharp shoulder, twisted in tangles of heavy, wet, copper hair, which encased a face of familiar beauty; soulful luminous eyes sheltered beneath a solid black line of shiny lashes, a dainty nose drawn to a small point and sweet toffee lips, parted slightly into a smile.

"Tempestas…" Arik's voice split as he choked back the lump that suddenly formed in his throat. A chunky tear oozed from one eye as he fought to hold back more. "I thought-"

"Shhh," Tempestas hushed her love with her velvety voice. "Go, quick, then come meet me at the cave." She handed the bracelet to Arik and he briefly embraced her frosty hand with his own. Suddenly, a scream sounded from behind him.

Arik spun round to see Grace gripping his mother by her hair and holding something shiny and sharp to her throat. To Arik's surprise, the soldiers were all tied up now, but Grace must have woken while Vivienne was working on getting her tied up too.

"You won't hurt her," Arik commanded sternly. He wasn't entirely sure himself whether he meant because he wouldn't allow it or if he meant because Grace needed his mum. Either way, the weapon Grace was brandishing was not entering his mother's throat.

"Ahh but you see Arik, I don't really *need* her. Your little sister should have everything I need. Your mum is just a bonus! So I suggest you and your little fishy friend back off before I push this knife into her," Grace refocused her demented glare on to Penelope, "and you Penelope. Put the baby back in the crib, nice and slowly." Penelope gazed down at the tiny baby in her arms. Then she whispered something that startled everyone, "she's asleep." She looked up from Terra at the room of wide terror-filled eyes glaring at her. "She's asleep," she repeated, but louder, "if I put her back in that cold hard cube she'll wake and scream. I can't do that to her. Grace, I would rather pass her straight to you." Grace eyed Penelope with a bemused expression smacked across her face. Arik figured she was probably shocked that someone considered her to possess '*warmth*'. After what felt like minutes, Grace finally spoke, "I can't have it screaming when I have work to do, pass it here." Grace kept the small knife to Vivienne's throat until the very last second when she could no longer hold it in place in order to take the baby. The transaction of baby from Penelope to Vivienne was just about to complete when Penelope suddenly snatched Terra right back and kicked Grace hard in the stomach with a force that sent her flying to the floor.

"Vivienne!" Penelope bent down to Vivienne's level and swiftly handed her the baby.

"Go!" she yelled, at both Arik and Vivienne, before pouncing onto a winded Grace, who was already almost motionless on the floor. Arik turned to make eye contact with Tempestas once last time, "I'll find you," he promised, then darted over to his mother and sister, guiding them hurriedly to the exit.

23

As soon as Penelope had witnessed Arik and his family leave the room safely, she turned her attention to Grace, who she now had strapped to the bed that Vivienne had occupied just moments earlier. She'd lost consciousness from the blow Penelope had dealt to her stomach. The shackles round her wrists were tightened so much that deep crimson lines began to run across her wrists and her hands were tinted purple. Her glasses were already smashed from Tempestas' tail whipping her against the wall, so Penelope removed them. Her eyes looked small and pathetic without the glasses emphasising their soullessness. Her jet-black hair was distressed and reaching out in all directions – not sitting in its usual immaculate poker-straight style. She looked, for once, helpless. Penelope almost began to feel something for her in that moment. Perhaps sadness, perhaps sympathy. But then she thought about Sam. She thought about the rotting dentist chair she'd found him on, saturated in layers of thick, congealing, scarlet liquid that spilled over to the floor because the chair simply could not soak up any more blood. She thought of the all the poor men in the wards with cable-tied mouths – black plastic weaving between holes in their top and bottom lips. She thought about the bruises and cuts she'd spied on Vivienne and shivered at the thought of what baby Terra might have been subjected to. She thought about Sam's legs – or the space where his legs used to be; short mouldy stumps, putrid and infecting until she'd saved him from certain death. With all these thoughts igniting pure rage inside her, Penelope kicked the brakes off the bed, wheeled it to the pool, snapped open the shackles that held Grace in place and let her slide into the depths. As she sunk, almost out of sight, a black shape swirled round her body and closed in. With greater speed, it pulled her body down further until she was out of sight. Penelope stared for a few minutes more. Eventually, a flood of opaque red began to rise and spread through the water like ink soaking into a page. Grace's chapter was over.

∎∎

24

After successfully escaping the S.T.A.B. building, Arik guided his mother and his baby sister back down the road that himself and Penelope had walked up earlier. He instructed his mother to follow him in and out of buildings regularly so they were never in view of anyone for more than thirty seconds or so – he figured a small boy carrying a baby and running down the street with a crazed looking woman in a hospital nightie would arouse some suspicion here on The Mainland. It wasn't long until the great, glass, glinting building, that held his brother, came within reach. He gave a meaningful nod towards the building that suggested to Vivienne that that's where Kai was. She nodded back and the two stepped out into the road. Suddenly, the doors to the front of the building whooshed open and piles of soldiers came spilling out. Arik and Vivienne jumped back and hid round the side of a shop.

"Shit, what is happening?!" Arik spat under his breath. His mum glanced at him in a way that would've resulted in a scalding had they been in any other situation – but in that moment it did not seem like the most important thing. There was no Kai, or Sam, in sight so he imagined they were still safe and undetected by soldiers. When Arik looked more carefully, he realised that the soldiers looked panicked and Arik soon realised they had picked up pace and were marching, almost jogging, back towards S.T.A.B. They must have been informed of what had happened in there just moments before. Arik was running out of time.

Arik dragged his mother across the road, into the building and worked the lift (to both his own and his mother's bewilderment). Soon they were on the top floor. The lift doors slid open and Arik spilled out, ran to the door of Penelope's apartment and began rapping on it frantically.

"Kai! Kai, it's me!" He called desperately. Suddenly the door swung open and Kai's tiny little face and large brown eyes beamed up at him. Arik bent down and scooped him into his arms with baby Terra. Vivienne began to weep with happiness.

"Mum!" Kai cried. He shuffled away from his brother and sister and ran over to embrace his mother. Soon, Sam emerged in a wheelchair.

"We have to move," Arik stated sharply, "Penelope stayed behind to deal with Grace, and now soldiers seem to be becoming aware of the situation." A flash of pain crossed Sam's tired face. But he understood their hurry.

"Go," he hushed, deeply and softly, "I'll wait here for Penelope."

"No!" Kai yelped. "You can't. They will find you and they will kill you." Arik knew Kai was right. He was fairly sure Sam knew it too. But Sam sat unwavering.

"Penelope saved my life, I can't just abandon her," he gulped.

"Sam, Penelope isn't coming back," Arik lied. Well, he wasn't sure if he was lying or not, but he had to say it to get Sam to move. Something in Sam's voice reminded him of his father, and he knew that Kai felt it too, he wasn't letting another person die today.

Eventually, and reluctantly, Sam agreed to leave the apartment. The five of them piled back into the lift and descended the cold building, Vivienne pushing Sam, Arik carrying Terra and Kai concentrating on keeping up himself.

After what seemed like a lifetime, they reached the water's edge. The guard towers were unmanned but various shouts, alarms and gunshots were ringing out from further inland. Everyone was drastically preoccupied. Chaos grew from S.T.A.B. and began to spread like wildfire. It wouldn't be long before it consumed every edge of the land while it searched for its prey. They didn't have long at all. "Over there!" yelled Sam. Somehow, from his seated position, he'd managed to spot the tip of a sail bobbing over the rocks. Hastily, Kai began to scramble up the rocks, followed by Vivienne who was clinging her daughter with one hand and the dry grey stone with her other hand. Arik surveyed the rocks in front of them then analysed Sam's wheelchair. Sam must have caught his scrutiny.

"I told you," he whispered, "just leave me."

"Nobody is leaving you anywhere!" A voice rang out in response to Sam – but it wasn't Arik's. The pair of them twisted their head rounds to see a drained Penelope, puffing and exasperated, hauling her tired limbs and red face towards them.

"Penelope…" Sam whimpered with a gentle blend of shock and delight. A smile brightened his previously gloomy faced as he admired the thin, pale, freckly woman, who'd saved his life, approach his wheelchair with some secret inner strength.

"We don't have much time, let's go," Penelope gestured towards the rocks before clasping one side of Sam's wheelchair, Arik grabbed the other and, by some incredible feat, the two dragged Sam up and over the smooth jagged rocks and set him down in the boat the other side. Kai, Vivienne and Terra were all already sat and ready to go. Arik was the last to board. He clambered in and pushed away from the rocks with one mighty blow. The Mainland quickly drifted away from them and Arik turned to begin rowing. He didn't look back. Silence hugged the small boat. Arik just rowed and rowed and rowed.

25

The rest of the day and one whole night passed. The Mainland was well and truly out of sight and the sun was just starting to peek over the horizon. A slim golden semi-circle cut into the dusky sky emitting warm rays that spliced the salty slate sea from the airy marshmallow sky. It felt comforting. Arik took this private moment to scour the water's surface. The yellow sun rays illuminated every ridge of wave, every ripple of a fish, every swirl in current. But it did not reveal the one thing Arik was looking for. Tempestas. Where was she? Arik had never spent this long at sea without her showing up. His heart shivered despite the warm sun rays crisping his salt-dried skin. Arik remained the only one awake until the sun was at least half emerged from the water. Everyone else began waking at roughly the same time and all looked equally exhausted; Sam looked as frail as always, Kai's bones were poking further from his body than usual, Penelope looked gaunt and pasty and his mother, his poor mother, was bent over, still asleep, with tiny Terra latched on to one of her breasts beneath her shabby gown. Vivienne's skin was dark and wrinkled like worn leather and bones protruded from her neck and collar. Arik felt a ball form in his throat as he gazed at his weak and feeble mother. "We need a plan," he croaked before clearing his throat to continue, "we are safe out here on the water," he gestured to his bracelet, "but we need food and, ironically, water." He glanced at Penelope who had her arms wrapped around Sam's slouched shoulders. He was praying she had a plan.

"I've no idea," she sighed, and her gaze fell to the floor of the boat. Then she noticed that at one end of the boat sat a solid trunk with a broken old latch. She sidled over to the box and opened it for some kind of hope, some kind of inspiration, but all that was inside was a few small saucepans, some old sheets of plastic and a few other bits of camping style equipment. Penelope sighed as she lowered the lid and further silence filled their ears. Not even Kai spoke. Arik gazed at his mother again. Her hair was brittle and clumps of salt had formed in the cracks of her skin. Dehydration was ringing her out like an old cloth. Soon she would not even be able to produce milk for Terra. For half a second, Arik considered whether they had all done the right thing, before quickly shaking his head while recollecting the horrors of The Mainland. For once, Arik felt more sad than angry. The blue bubbles of sadness that bounced between his bones quelled the otherwise roaring red anger. He felt helpless. He felt like a failure.

"Dad would have been so proud of us for rescuing Mummy and Terra," Kai smiled. It was as if Kai could see Arik's feelings. The bubbles of sadness now crept up his body and flooded his face, causing an intense build up behind his eyes. He pulled Kai into his chest so he wouldn't see him cry. Suddenly, a plop that resembled a large round pebble being dropped into water, echoed from behind Kai. Arik peered over his small shoulder to see a large rippling effect expanding from a centre point near the boat, evidence he hadn't imagined it. To further reinforce faith in his own senses, Penelope had suddenly clambered over from the other side of the boat too.

"Did you see what it was?" she asked, desperation lacing her voice.

"No," Arik replied, but then he smiled. It had to be… surely… Another plop sounded to right of them. They turned quick enough this time to catch a flick of a tail ducking beneath the water.

"Tempestas!" Arik cried with glee. He beamed an incredible smile as he darted to the edge of the boat and leant right over until his face was almost touching the water. "Tempestas, oh my, I'm so, so glad you found us –" Suddenly two large hands burst from the dark indigo liquid beneath Arik's face and clasped him by the sides of the head. But they weren't female hands. The two chunky, masculine hands gripped with immense power before forcing Arik over the edge of the boat.

■ ■

"ARIK!" Penelope and Vivienne yelled in unison. "What on earth is that!?" screamed Penelope. Kai went to immediately jump in after his brother but Penelope just caught him. "Don't be an idiot!" she shouted at him. "Arik! ARIK! Oh god. What are we going to do?" She turned to face Sam and Vivienne.

"I have an idea," Sam answered her rapidly, "but it involves you getting in there too."

"Whatever it takes," Penelope rushed back to him.

"Go down and help Arik fight it off, try to get him up for air, when the thing resurfaces, I will deal with it." He glanced down to a long pole that ran down the side of him along the bottom of the boat. It was a spear. Kai jumped to his feet and helped pass the spear to Sam while Penelope launched into the water with no further words.

The cool indigo was quite welcoming against Penelope's blistering red skin. She had no time to enjoy the sensation though. She kicked and twisted and flicked herself round in the water in search for Arik and the monster in the endless blue. But it wasn't endless. Not far below her was the sea bed! Thoughts of how this was possible when they were so far out began to enter her mind when she suddenly spied two white bodies and a fish tail in a tussle against the floor below. She bombed down through the water at lightning speed and wrapped her bony arms round the thick throat of the beast that was pinning down Arik. Arik squirmed and kicked and wriggled free before dealing the thing an almighty blow to its hairless face with the heel of his foot. He used the force of it to propel himself back to the surface for air. Penelope clung on. She tried to tighten her grip round the creature's broad neck, but she was losing strength. The powerful fish tail whipping around her was weakening her further. Her skinny white arms gripped over his boulder-like shoulders that bulged out further than where her elbows reached. He was solid. His skin was a bullet proof layer of leather, shielding rows of rocks beneath. For a brief second, Penelope compared the feeling to how Sam's slumped shoulders had felt beneath her arms moments earlier. It saddened her to think he would have once been as strong as the beast she clung to now, but she quickly reminded herself that she'd saved him from becoming this mutant. Her muted ears caught bubbles of sound as she scrambled around on the seabed floor looking for something. A rock. Anything. Soon her hand ran over an old brick. She brought it above her head and smashed it into the skull of the beast as brutally as she could through the waters resistance. Her small arms were unable to put a lot of force behind the brick, but the creature's tail ceased to flick suddenly so Penelope shot frantically back up through the water with all the speed she could muster. She soon burst through the surface and Arik and Kai pulled her into the boat in one swift smooth action. Suddenly, without even a moment in it, the creature soared out from the water right behind her, launching towards them. As it flew over, time seemed to slow and Arik studied the mans fearless face. There was no hair, not even evidence of a closely shaved beard. He didn't have any eyebrows or any hair on his head, just a smooth peach top. Two crystal grey eyes glared down into the boat. Arik noticed these last, before time seemed to speed up again, but he could've sworn it had no pupils. Suddenly, it reached out its hands to grab Penelope but they instantly fell limp inches from her face; simultaneously, a sharp metal sound like a knife being drawn from a sheath sliced the sky. Hot sticky blood rained down on them as the dead beast finished its descent into the water the other side of the boat – a spear sticking out from deep beneath its left ribs.

A silence swathed the boat once more – but not an awkward one; it was more of a limbo moment of astonishment and relief. Eventually, it was Sam who spoke first.

"I guess that was what Grace had destined for me; a soldier in her own underwater army. But why did it come after us? I thought the idea was to send them after Femaestus."

"They're still under the command of Grace, she's probably sent them out to find us," Arik replied. Penelope gulped. She knew it couldn't be Grace herself commanding them anymore but perhaps Arik was right in that they were still under some sort of command from The Mainland armies. How could they have all been so foolish to think escaping on a boat was a good idea – where were they going to go? There was nowhere to hide in the vast open blue. "We will just have to keep rowing until we find a solution, Arik. Arik?" He did not respond to Penelope. She turned to find him ogling the ocean, mouth agape and eyes dilated. "Arik? What is it?" Penelope began to panic. They had used their only weapon and let it sink to the depths with the dead fish beast – although it couldn't be too far from the boat. Just as Penelope opened her mouth to declare she was going back in to find the spear, Arik spoke, "Tempestas!!"

This time it really was her. Her hair of liquid gold clung flat to her small round scalp as she bobbed gently towards them in the water. Her beauty infused the air with a rich sweet scent that softened the salty smell that surrounded them. The sun, still not fully risen from its watery slumber, encased her in a succulent syrup glow. Pearls of water ran down her tender milky skin, guarded from entering her emerald eyes by her voluminous oily lashes. She was breath-taking. Arik felt a crippling crimson warmth grip his heart. It weakened him. He had felt this before when he was with Tempestas but the hold it had over him grew stronger each time. Tempestas reached the boat and rested her elbows and hands up on the edge. Arik immediately leaned in and kissed her. Vivienne looked on with bewilderment, still breastfeeding Terra. Her facial expressions, while showing complete shock, were also entwined with some kind of acceptance. Whether it was because she hadn't the energy to ask questions or whether it was just because nothing surprised her anymore, Arik was not sure. One thing he was sure of however was that his mum was getting more and more sick and dehydrated by the minute. Her eyelids were closing heavily over her chalky yellow eyes.

"Look! There's more!" Kai suddenly yelped. Behind Tempestas were now about fifty beautiful faces dotted about in the water. Kai was clearly excited by the view but Arik felt a little wary.

"Don't worry," Tempestas soothed him with her caramel tones, "we're all here to help." She flashed a brilliant white smile that almost knocked Arik off his feet. "Not far below you is the land of an old flooded country, people assume the entire country is gone but if you go in far enough, there's a small piece of land left above sea level. It's quite far out – so far that nobody from The Mainland has ever been there - we're going to take you." A tidal wave of hope splashed down into the small boat and washed over the six previously hopeless souls. They all took a moment to bask in it. Smiles flitted between them and everybody's eyes lit up. Except Vivienne's, whose eyes were now completely shut.

"We have to move quick," Arik pleaded, "my mum isn't going to make it." As soon as the words left his mouth he realised he should have chosen them more carefully, for now Kai was glaring up at him with worried eyes, as wide as the sun itself. A tear escaped from one of them. "It's ok Kai, she'll be fine as long as we get going soon." Kai nodded to convey understanding although Arik wasn't even sure if he really believed him. Arik turned back to Tempestas and the other Fems but they had all relocated. Many were stationed at the back of the boat and the rest were dispersed evenly around them like bodyguards.

"You all ready?" Tempestas grinned, "hold on tight." And with that, the boat shot through the water like a war-bound torpedo.

The tired boat eventually came to rest in a bed of thick black mud which made for the edge of the island. Despite the speed they had been travelling at, the journey had seemed to last a lifetime. Arik was sure it only felt this way because every second that dripped past was a second closer to his mum giving up. Still, he wondered how far out they had voyaged. The Femaestus wedged the boat so it was steady but only so half of it was on land with the other half still partially submerged. Arik was the first to disembark. His feet sank slightly into the squelching sludge. The mud was warm and the air was fresh with the zesty petrichor that rose from the drier ground further in land. Two creamy yellow butterflies tumbled past Arik before disappearing into the trees ahead. The shallow waves lashing at the land edge made the only sound. They crashed against the sand with each harsh push in land and washed back out equally as garishly. The sea's clear hands grasping at the muddy floor reminded Arik of desperation. The crisp scent of salt-lined sea-air curled through the sky and cooled their nostrils and lungs. The sun fried the shoulders of the six survivors while the few Femaestus, who were still bobbing around in the water, seemed to bask in its formidable heat. Penelope had lifted Terra from Vivienne's limp arms, while Arik had been taking in their surroundings, and passed her sweet small body to Sam. Sam curled his loving arms around her and Terra breathed a happy sigh. Arik and Penelope then turned to Vivienne who was now slumped right over on top of herself. They hooked their arms beneath hers and hauled her roughly from the boat. The splintered wood rasped against the thin flesh on her back but she didn't wince. Arik and Penelope dragged her into the trees and sat her up in the shade.

"Where do we get water?" Penelope's arid throat croaked at Arik. He racked his brains for all of five seconds before remembering the camping equipment in the trunk on the boat.

"The stuff on the boat – I can make some kind of water desalination equipment using it. We had to do it quite often on out on the stilts if The Mainland didn't give dad enough water to bring home." Arik's voice broke. He had barely even thought about Morgan since the night on the raft. The night – Arik shook his head. This still wasn't the time to properly grieve his father – nor would it be what his father would want right now. When Morgan's heart used to beat, it beat for Vivienne. Arik knew that. He knew his dad loved him and Kai. But nothing compared to the way his heart swelled with adoration for his mother. He worshipped her. To see her like this now, near death, would have been enough to destroy him. Arik had to save his mother. He raced back to the boat, snatched the items from the trunk and began assembling it to create a form of water desalination apparatus.

Later in the day, after everyone had quenched their thirst slightly with an insubstantial amount of water, Arik decided to venture further into the trees on the small spec of land they now occupied. Vivienne had come back to life some (owing mostly to everyone donating most of their share of water to her) and was resting beneath a shady tree, breastfeeding Terra again. Kai was sat at the edge of the water, trying to stab small fish with a half blunt stick. Penelope and Sam were chatting and chuckling together equidistant from both Vivienne and Kai, as if still protecting them both. Arik knew everybody was safe now and so he took the opportunity to explore his new surroundings.

Arik stepped past his mother and brushed aside the first curtain of juicy green leaves that hung down to the floor. Behind them, as Arik had expected, were further velvety green curtains, draping round various thick pillars of tree trunk, from canopy to ground. The vines and leaves were twisted and entwined and wild. The thickness grew the deeper he ventured, to a point where Arik almost felt like he would soon be unable to go any further. He did however manage to tear back one more sheet of snaking vines with his raw hands to reveal a beautiful, warm, open space smiling at him on the other side. As he pulled down the final curtain, an abundance of birds took flight. The raucous clap of wings startled him initially, but within seconds it became a harmonious combination of melodious tweets, echoing around the vast plane. The sun continued to radiate down on Arik's crisp face yet he lifted his head to embrace it some more. He stretched his arms out, smiled and allowed the greenness that surrounded him to heal his skin, flush through his veins and oxygenate his airways. He felt at one with the earth on which he stood. He felt the power from the ground flow between his toes. He felt, for the first time in a long time, safe. After taking a moment for himself he then scampered back through the bushes to the outer clearing.

"Come on you guys, let's get deeper inland. There's a beautiful space this way. Let's go!" He nodded at

Penelope to affirm he had Sam ready to lift on his side. She returned the gesticulation and they lifted in perfect timing. They headed to the gap in the bush that Arik had created, followed closely by Kai who held Terra in one arm and supported his mother with the other.

26

Weeks passed. They hadn't quite been on the island for a month, but two or three weeks had definitely passed. Arik wasn't keeping count. Instead he had been enjoying life for a while; tickling and teaching his baby sister, talking to and appreciating his mother and playing and exploring, like normal brothers, with Kai. He'd increased the production of the water desalination and together they were keeping well fed on various fruits, fish and even the odd bird if they manage to catch one. Sometimes Tempestas bought them gifts; a scrumptious salmon here, a tantalising tuna there. But food was not the only treat Tempestas regularly salvaged from the sea. As well as delicious delicacies, Tempestas also brought to the island various pieces of furniture. All were slimy and algae ridden when they first arrived. Some dried in the sun to reveal wood so old and mouldy it just splintered and crumbled to pieces. However, other pieces were remarkable. A few ornate old chairs that looked like they once belonged in a public house, a sturdy rocking chair, and a large family size picnic table now sat in the sun on the island. They even had a few bed frames between them which they had lined with grass filled plastic bags which there were plenty of floating around in the water. But Arik's favourite thing by far was the tiny cot Tempestas had recovered for Terra. She had even acquired a small cushion and blanket to line it, but she never said where she had gotten those. Arik was sure they hadn't been submerged in water for twenty years, nor was he sure he even cared. His sister had comfort, his family had safety and he had Tempestas. Every day he sat by the waters edge and they talked for hours. Regularly, Arik joined her in the water and they would go for swims together. His favourite moments were evenings when the twilight sun would illuminate her golden skin and cause the scales on her tail to sparkle and shimmer in a soft, enchanting jade. He would stroke her arms and back and trail his fingers right down her spine to where skin became scales, and still he would continue. Her tail was strikingly rigid. Each individual scale was around an inch thick and layered upon two or three other discs. They were oddly dry, despite how much they glistened and twinkled wetly in the setting sun. Tempestas would stretch out on the mud in the evenings, where the water overlapped the earth. It reminded Arik how half of her belonged in the sea and the other half belonged on land… with him. She would extend her arms, reaching out into the clear water above her head, which was only an inch or two deep. She would arch her back until it left the water and her ribs thrust from beneath her skin. And she would flex her tail, her magnificent tail, as she pushed out, her caudal fins would unfold and flop heavily into the thin layer of water, although they were barely submerged, the thick emerald layer that rested above the water shone with blinding brightness. Various dainty tassel-like embellishments dangled down into the shallow pools around her. No words came to Arik in those beautiful evening moments. No words could do them justice. And there were no words to describe how he felt for Tempestas. He would just savour every precious moment with her, before turning in to sleep… alone.

One such evening, Arik was sitting at the waters edge, gently freeing seaweed from Tempestas' tangled scalp, when a distant hum whirred from far out at sea. At first Arik thought it might be the echo of a storm rolling in from afar but as the sound continued, and increased quickly in volume, he soon realised that it was no storm; instead, panic surged through his body like a strike of lightning as he recognised the familiar sound of speedboats approaching.

"Kai, put the fire out!" Without question, Kai fetched some water and tossed it over the blaze so only dim embers remained. The sun had just dipped below the horizon and the humming of the boats seemed louder in the darkness but still not visible. The sky and sea were robed in matching navy blue and Arik could still make out the faintly glowing pallor of everyone's faces. His breath spiralled from his lungs as he tried to remain calm. Suddenly, the engine whirrs ceased. Arik sucked in his chest. Kai glanced at him worriedly. The whole night stood deathly still. Then, just as he began to think they were safe, Tempestas screeched from the waters edge. Arik spun round. Two large hands had grasped her body and were dragging her furiously into the water. Her tail flapped and smashed and she whipped her body round and round like a fish out of water but it was no use. The two hands pulled her all too easily into the water. Suddenly a second screeching sound sliced the salty night air. Arik turned back the other way to see Penelope arched over Sam, cradling his limp torso; then Arik noticed the arrow in his chest.

"Into the forest, now! Go!" Arik roared thunderously. Vivienne fled into the trees, Terra bundled in her protective arms, while Kai grabbed Penelope by the shoulders, trying to pull her in the same direction. Another arrow whizzed through the air and penetrated the dirt next to Kai's feet.

"Come *on*, Penelope!" He begged. Reluctantly, she dropped Sam's lifeless body to the floor and followed Kai into the bushes. Arik knew immediately he had to stop whoever this was attacking them before they reached the land – but he couldn't do that without Tempestas. He sprinted for the ocean. The icy moon had spilled milky moonlight over the sea now and Arik could just make out two or three silhouettes of speedboats in the distance. He dived in. He began to swim. He hoped his eyes would adjust to the faintly lit water, but he could barely see. Suddenly, something grasped him by the waist. Small hands. Dainty hands. Before he knew it, he was being kissed forcefully on the lips. Instantly, his vision became clear. The black ocean illuminated with untraceable light and burst into a soft pastel blue. Bobbing in front of him, with a face full of fear, was Tempestas. Her right cheek was slashed, and bruises marred her formerly seamless skin. She pushed back from Arik, parted her lips and began to sing. A mesmerising song curled through the thin water. Her velvet voice was made from creamy cashmere and silky satin and it swaddled Arik's soothed body. But he was not enchanted, merely relaxed.

"That should keep them entranced up there for a while, but first, we need to deal with this." Tempestas floated aside to reveal an army of dark eyes, ribbed torsos and vast waving tails approaching, A man-made army... of male Femaestus. To Arik's relief, hundreds of actual Femaestus began to emerge from the depths and surround himself and Tempestas protectively. Within seconds, bodies catapulted through the water like heavy torpedoes. Rows of human missiles slammed together, male on female. Masculine roars and feminine shrieks bounced off each other, filling the sea with belligerent war cries. The snap of bones breaking, the jerk of hair whipping and the sight of skin slashing formed a deathly scene of chaos before. One by one, various bodies attached to colossal tails sank into the darkness below. Then Arik felt a sensational pain, like a thousand whips, strike him across the back. He spiralled through the water, dazed, the skin on his back stinging in the salt water. He looked back to see the zombie-like face of a man reeling towards him. He couldn't move as fast as they could in the water. Suddenly, he was yanked downwards and the male Femaestus flew right above his head, crashing headfirst into another. Both bodies tumbled down beside him, their tails swirling into the darkness below like water spinning down a plug. Below him another fight was taking place; two huge tails batting and whipping and slashing, flashes of green and blue and gold glinting through the water. The strength of the tails caused ripples so forceful that Arik soon found himself being propelled towards the surface. He tried to push his way back down but it was futile. He burst through the surface of the water where he suddenly heard voices. A disc of light darted about the choppy waves around him. Right next to him now was one of the speedboats. Arik clambered up the back on board. The three men with the torch were all looking out in to the sea in the opposite direction. Arik knew he wouldn't be able to take on all three so, with some vain sense of hope and belief, he yelled for Tempestas. The moment the men turned to face him,

Tempestas came soaring out of the water. She flew through the air as gracefully as an angel, then wiped out the three men with her demonic tail. Water poured into the boat as a result of the wave Tempestas created when re-entering the sea. Arik splashed through to get the engine started. The other speedboats were now under attack by the other Femaestus – it seemed as though they had won their sublevel battle. Arik smiled and began steering back towards the land. The boat wedged up on the shore and Arik ran up and through the trees into the clearing.

"Mum? Kai? Arik called, at first triumphantly, but at the lack of response his cries became more desperate. "Mum? Penelope? Kai?" Where were they? The piece of land was so small. There was nowhere else to go and certainly nowhere else to hide…

There was nowhere else to hide.

Arik sprinted back to the waters edge and called for Tempestas again.

"How many boats were there?" Arik asked, more viciously than he intended. "How many boats were there?!" he repeated, this time louder.

"I'm not sure," Tempestas replied, breathless and exhausted, "three?"

"Four. There were four. They had one round the other side of the island. Mum, Penelope, Kai and Terra. They're gone."

Arik's anger melted into sadness as he slumped down into the boggy waters edge. Tempestas hauled her tail up into the sludge and placed an arm round Arik's sagging shoulder.

"We will find them," she reassured him. The pain that antagonised the skin on Arik's back returned to him; burning and raw. Soon Tempestas would have to return to the water and Arik would be left alone. The future of his family and possibly all human existence rested in the hands of his mother and his baby sister and he felt entirely useless. But, as he glanced around the shore and saw Sam's dead half-body laying cold and still in the moonlight, he knew exactly what he had to do.

153

Printed in Great Britain
by Amazon